THE BLUE FEATHER

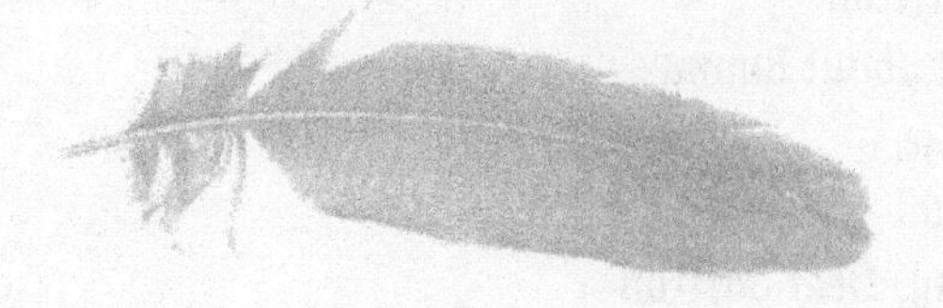

Also by Gary Crew

Novels

Strange Objects
The Inner Circle
The House of Tomorrow
No Such Country
Angel's Gate
Edward Britton
The Truth about Emma
Dark House
Force of Evil
Dear Venny, Dear Saffron
Plague of Quentaris

Sam Silverthorne

Quest
Menace
Victory

Picture Books

Memorial
Beneath the Surface
The Lost Diamonds of Killiecrankie
The Rainbow
The Lantern
Young Murphy
The Viewer

THE BLUE FEATHER

GARY CREW MICHAEL O'HARA

LOTHIAN

A Lothian Children's Book

This edition published in Australia and New Zealand in 2015
by Hachette Australia
(an imprint of Hachette Australia Pty Limited)
Level 17, 207 Kent Street, Sydney NSW 2000
www.hachettechildrens.com.au

First published in 1997 by Mammoth Australia
Republished in 2002 by Hodder Headline Australia

National Library of Australia
Cataloguing-in-Publication data:

Crew, Gary, author.
The blue feather/Gary Crew, Michael O'Hara.

978 0 7336 1075 2 (paperback)

O'Hara, Michael.

A823.3

Text design by Tony Gilevski
Cover design by Mathematics
Typeset in Quadraat by Bookhouse, Sydney
Printed and bound in Australia by Griffin Press, Adelaide,
an Accredited ISO AS/NZS 14001:2009 Environmental Management System printer

The paper this book is printed on is certified against the Forest Stewardship Council® Standards. Griffin Press holds FSC chain of custody certification SGS-COC-005088. FSC promotes environmentally responsible, socially beneficial and economically viable management of the world's forests.

For my father and in memory of my mother

M. O'H.

For Helen Chamberlin, editor without peer

G. C.

'. . . we have not even to risk the adventure alone; or the heroes of all time have gone before us; the labyrinth is thoroughly known; we have only to follow the thread of the hero-path. And where we had thought to find an abomination, we shall find a god; where we had thought to slay another, we shall slay ourselves; where we had thought to travel outward, we shall come to the centre of our own existence; where we had thought to be alone, we shall be with all the world.'

Joseph Campbell, The Hero with a Thousand Faces

From the ship's log of the sealing vessel *Sea Harvest*

15th of September, 1801

This afternoon, while hunting the seal off the islands of the Recherche Archipelago, we were obliged to curtail our work, as a great bird swooped low over us, terrifying the crew and more than once gathering our catch in its mighty talons. Never have I seen such a bird. A sea eagle it may be, but of such enormous size that the span of its wings darkened the sun . . .

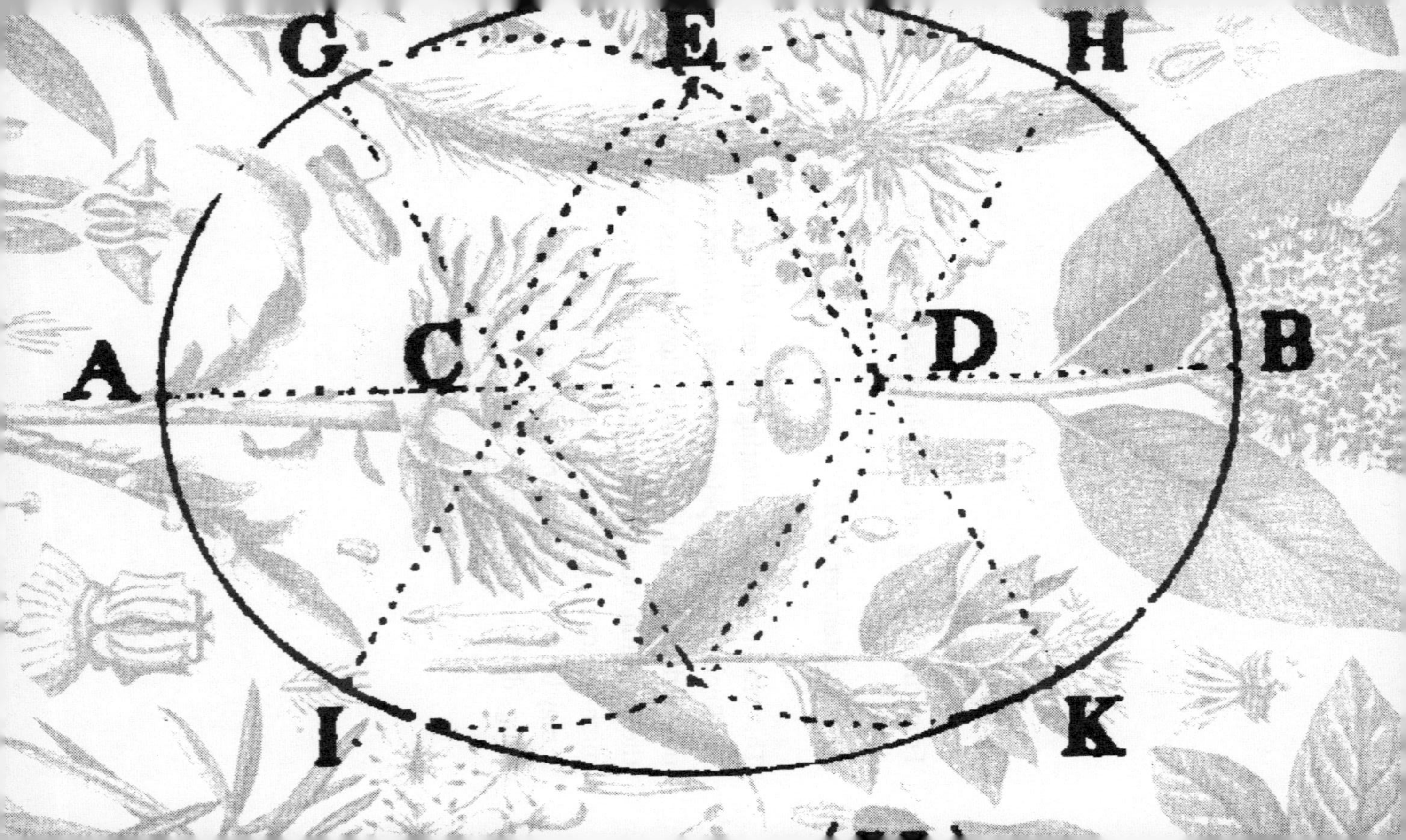
G
E
H
A
C
D
B
I
K

From the journal of Martin Abrahams, botanist, gathering specimens to the north of the Recherche Archipelago

18th of October, 1873

Of further interest was the discovery of the partial remains of an egg, buried in soft soil and decayed vegetation, at the furtherest end of the ravine. The size of this egg was astounding: nine inches in diameter and fifteen inches in length, although this latter dimension was approximated, as the specimen was incomplete, being shattered at its smaller end. To determine what creature, feathered or scaled, could have produced such an egg, defies the bounds of my knowledge and my imagination.

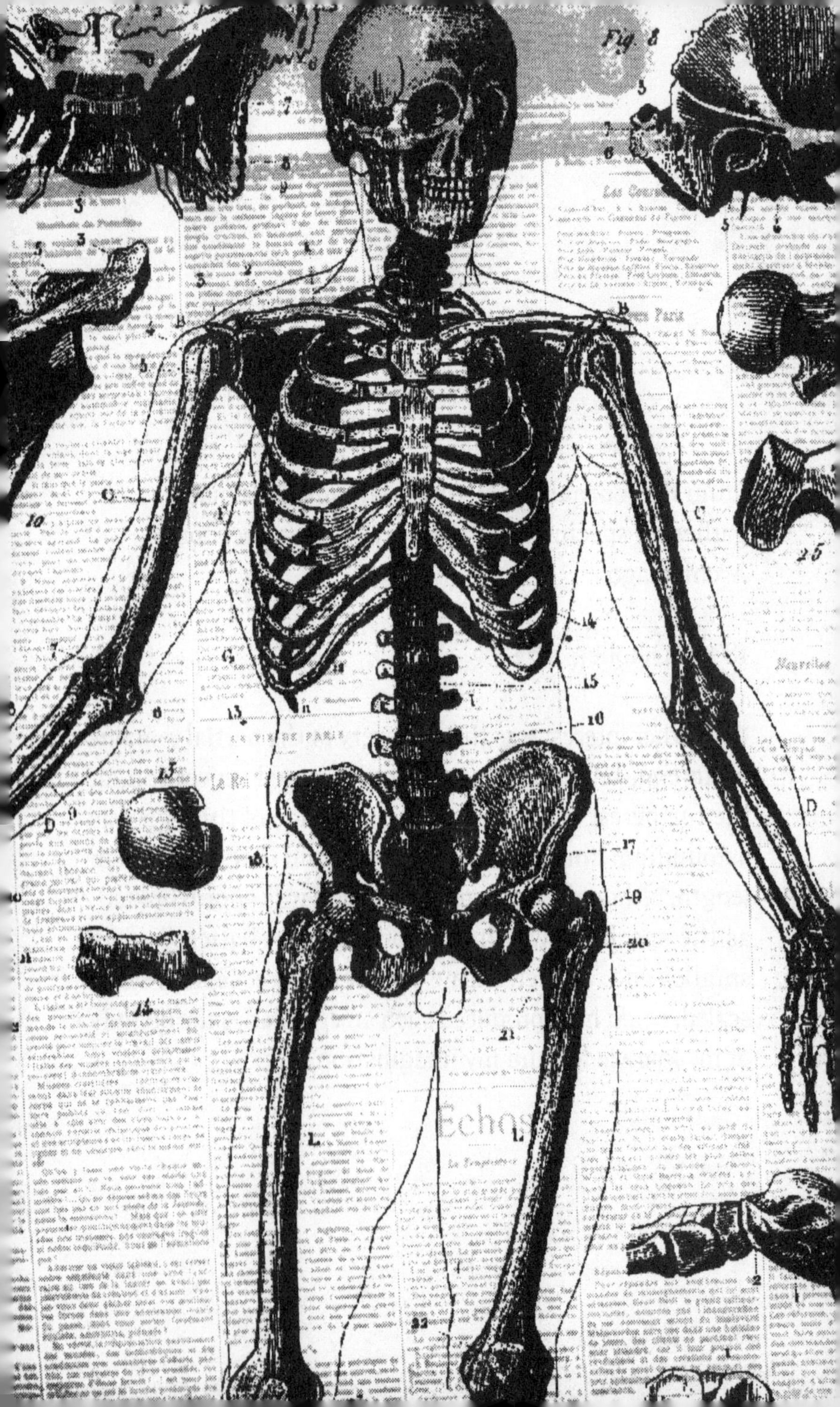

From *The Clarion*, 22 February, 1903

SAD NEWS FROM THE DESERT

Yesterday, trackers found the body of Mr Bernard Pearce, sapphire prospector, in a gully one hundred and fifty miles to the north of Esperance. Mr Pearce had been missing for three weeks, after he left his fellows to search for the elusive stones alone. It is said that the man's skull was covered by deep scratches, that could be the result of attack by a clawed or taloned creature. Sergeant Allen, of the Esperance Police, discounts such rumours. Mr Pearce's funeral will be held in St Matthew's Church, Queen Street, Esperance, at 10 a.m. tomorrow. The prospector leaves a wife and three children. A Charitable Collection will be taken at the service.

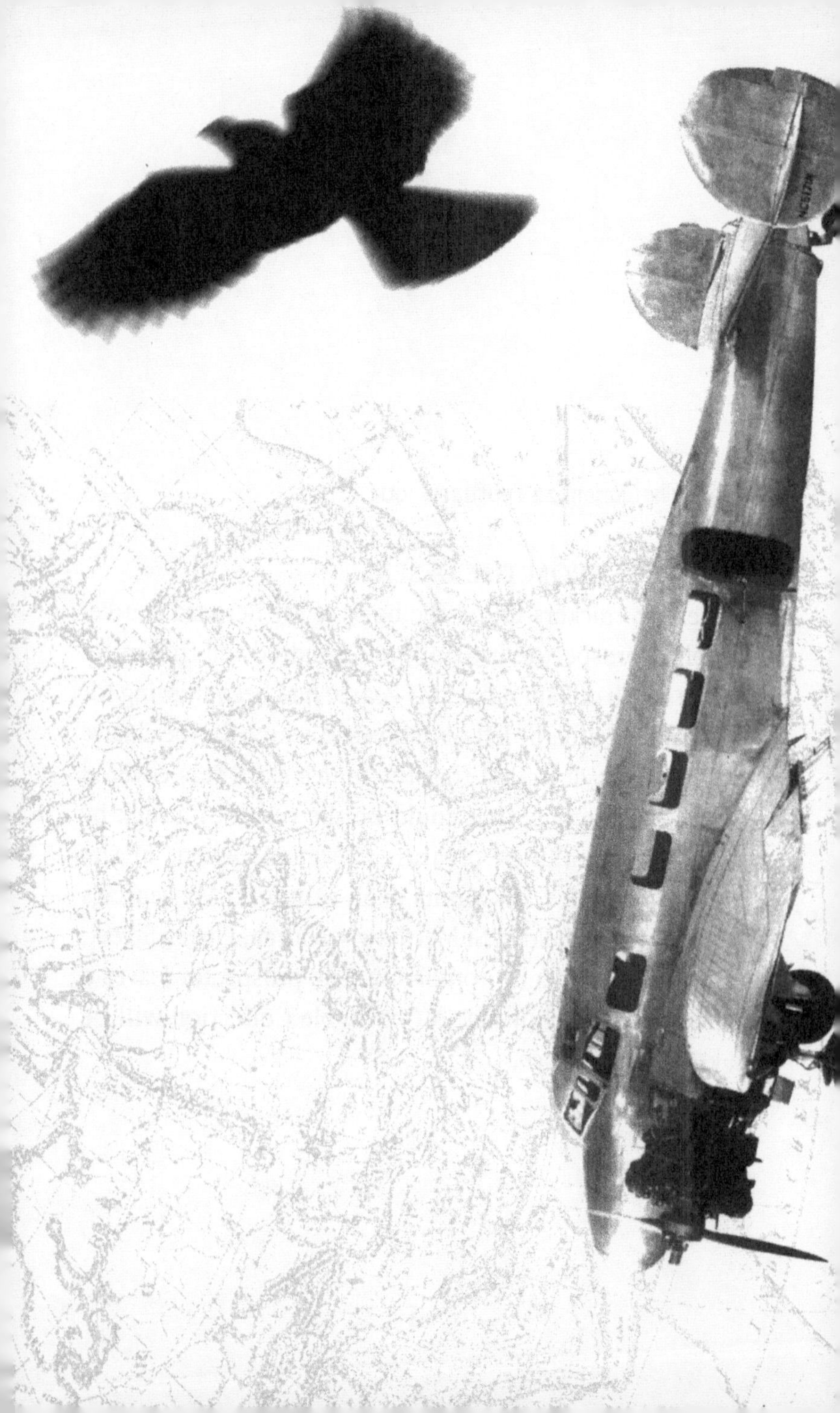

From Australian Airforce Despatches. 1400 hours.

22 September, 1942

DES. 233462. Mullaway single-engine fighter on routine training flight over Great Southern Ocean missing from formation of three. Group Captain Perrott reports sighting of fourth 'aircraft-size' shadow on the surface of the sea immediately before the loss. Confirmation to follow. Base.

PIX SENSATION

Excerpt from *Pix Sensation*, Christmas Edition, 1963

Oxbridge was at the wheel of the vehicle when his wife called 'Look out'. He said he automatically applied the brakes and stopped. In the sky about 50 metres in front of them was what appeared to be a giant, bird-like creature.

It was difficult to get details about the creature's size and shape from Oxbridge. He persisted in describing it as 'more of a colour', and referred to it as 'shimmering' or 'shining blue'. While it is true that both Oxbridge and his wife claim to have seen UFOS on several occasions, when they were interviewed separately their individual accounts still matched word for word. Either they have learnt them by heart or they really did see something distinctly alien out there in that desert. Who knows? What a pity they 'forgot' the camera, I say. (Ed.)

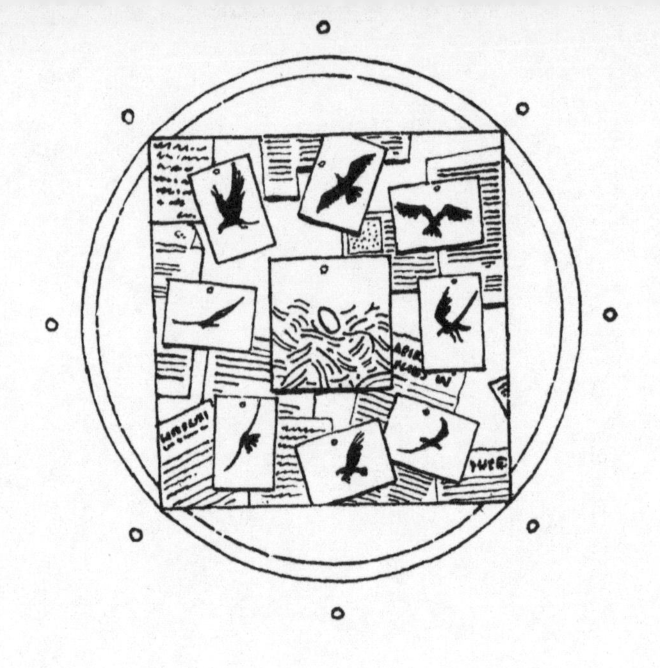

GRAHAM AND BURWOOD, the boy's counsellors, brought him to the Deep River Raptor Sanctuary about one in the afternoon. Greg Muir, the owner of the place, was taking his lunch break at a table out in the yard. He looked up to see the three of them standing there and recognised the men at once. He stood up, the sun brilliant behind him.

The counsellors shaded their eyes, but the boy grimaced and squinted. 'I can't see,' he said.

Then move,' Muir answered. 'I can't shift the sun.'

But the boy stayed where he was.

Later, as he always did when the events of the day had been squared away, Muir would record in his journal that even then, even as those first words were spoken, he thought that he heard the boy laugh. Not 'heard' exactly, he wrote, more 'sensed' that he had laughed. Or snickered. Like a threat, or a challenge . . .

If Muir prided himself on anything, it was that he could trust his senses. Still, he wouldn't have been surprised if the boy had laughed. He had known for over a week that Graham and Burwood were bringing him, and why. He should not have been taken aback by the proud arch of the boy's eyebrow and, beneath the lock of thick blond hair that fell across his forehead, the fixed and sightless stare of his left eye, dark brown, almost black, and made of glass.

According to the counsellors' report, the boy had lost his eye at the age of six. He was almost sixteen now, yet in all those years he had never told anyone how it had been lost. How, or why, or by whom it had been gouged, cut or poked from its socket. He had not told a single person. Not either of his parents, nor his doctors. And certainly not Graham or Burwood, his present custodians, who stood either side of him like guards flanking a prisoner.

After some shuffling and shoving so that he could see, Burwood cleared his throat and took the introductory plunge. 'Ah, Greg, this is Simon Meekam. Ah, Simon, this is Greg Muir, Manager of the Deep River Sanctuary, ah, Raptor Sanctuary. The Deep River Raptor Sanctuary.'

At this, Simon's right eye flickered, even rolled a little. As if, being one-eyed, he couldn't read the metre-high words burnt into the split-log gateway at the entrance to the place. As if he hadn't cocked his head sideways, like a bird, to focus his single eye and take in the message. As if he hadn't understood who Muir was for himself.

Burwood stumbled on. 'Simon, um . . . Greg's the one who's agreed to take you on . . . under his wing, so to speak. And if that works out, well, we've asked him to take you with him on . . . a sort of an . . . um . . . expedition that he's been planning . . . um . . . over Esperance way. Down south. Um . . . east . . .'

Now the boy laughed. A distinct chuckle burst from his throat. 'He can try,' he said.

Graham and Burwood exchanged glances. This was not a good start.

But Muir seemed equal to it. He set aside his coffee cup, wiped some crumbs from the corners of his mouth, folded his newspaper and stared straight at the boy. 'Mr Graham and Mr Burwood tell me that you don't want to go to school, but you can't hold a steady job either. That you run away all the time, which is the reason you're in State Care. Is that true?'

'Ah . . .' Burwood began, attempting to redress the situation, hoping to offer a fresh lead in, but the boy said, 'Sure I run. Wouldn't you?'

Muir gave this some thought. 'Not necessarily,' he said. 'Not necessarily . . . But tell me, Simon, since you read my signs, what's a sanctuary, exactly?'

The counsellors shuffled again, ready for trouble. Simon turned to look at them, letting them know that he could handle the situation without their help. 'I know what a sanctuary is,' he answered. 'And you must too, seeing you own the place, so why ask me to tell you what you already know?'

Muir smiled. 'To find out if you know, OK?'

In response, Simon planted his feet wide, folded his arms across his chest and said, 'A sanctuary could be a sacred place in a church or a temple . . . but knowing what Mr Graham and Mr Burwood told me – and what I can see for myself – I guess what you would call a sanctuary, Mr Muir, is a place where living things are protected. Like the birds of prey – the raptors – you've got caged up here. Been caught in traps, or shot, haven't they, so they can't fly properly, right?'

Muir glanced at the counsellors and then back at Simon. 'Yes,' he said. 'That's right.'

'Then I'd say that your friends here must have brought me to this place – this *sanctuary* – because they think I'm sick too. And you're going to help me get better. Going to keep me here, and when you think I've *recovered*, you might take me on this trip they've been talking about. You know, like one of those falcons they let fly on a lead . . .'

'More of a trek, Simon,' Muir corrected, calmly ignoring the boy's cynicism. 'But that remains to be . . .'

'OK. A trek then. But whatever it is, the idea is to keep me on the straight and narrow, hey?'

Now Muir smiled at him. 'No, Simon,' he said. 'My plans have got very little to do with you at all. In fact, you should consider yourself fortunate that your counsellors here even considered that I might allow you to come. At the moment, it seems that you would be little more than a liability.' Muir let this register, then, just as the boy was about to respond, added, 'But you look like you could use a favour.'

'Sure,' Simon sneered. 'I've heard it all before. You reckon that you're doing this stuff for my own good, but all the time you'll have your eye on me, hey, watching everything I do, every move I make . . . and then there's got to be a report, hasn't there? When I've done my time. At the end of the trip.' He used the word with deliberate defiance, aimed directly at Muir. 'That's when you really get to play God, hey? When you get to tell these guys about my behaviour. My progress. Shit, you must think I'm dumb.'

At this he gave a dismissive laugh and walked away, disappearing down one of the many pathways that meandered between the raptors' towering cages, leaving the others to stare after him.

He wandered for a while, chuckling to himself, until he came across a guided tour, a party of six or eight pensioners being shown the birds, and skirted around them. He spotted a low-set timber house and presumed that this was Muir's place. He saw a worker repairing a cage and noticed his khaki-coloured shorts and cotton shirt – the same as Muir's, the same as the tour guide's – and grimaced, guessing that this was the uniform he would be forced to wear.

At last he reached the limits of the sanctuary: one final cage at the end of an overgrown path. Satisfied that he was alone, he sat on a garden seat in the shade. Muir would come after him, he was certain. But not right away. First he would decide to make the boy wait, to teach him a lesson, then he would come. Conscience stricken or driven by guilt – the boy knew all the terms – but Muir would eventually come. The man would try to soothe him, to calm him down, then he would be shown the ropes, told how the place operated, and expected to turn up for work bright and happy the next day.

He smiled. He had been through this so many times. Sooner or later, maybe in a day or so, depending, he knew that he would leave. He knew that he would cut and run, like always. He smiled again and stretched, and was about to settle for a long wait, when a sound caught his attention. Like a muffled scream or a yelp, caught in the throat. He sat still and listened, hearing it quite clearly the second time. It came from the cage opposite, on the other side of the path.

He moved closer and peered through the wire. High up, in the gloomy shadows beneath the roof, he saw a solitary bird staring down at him. Being city-born and bred, and ignorant, he could only guess that it was an eagle. As he watched, it turned as if to see him better, as if to focus those great golden-brown eyes upon his own. And then it leaned forward a little, dipping its head as if in recognition. As if it knew him.

Suddenly afraid, Simon Meekam backed away.

Shane Rowe
Senior Editor
Rare Earth
PO Box 74
Perth WA

26 September

Dear Shane,

How was your holiday – I missed you! This is just a quick note to explain the enclosed tape. It's an update on the ground parrots and a proposal for a new project – I hope you like the idea. I'll talk to you (on tape) again soon.

Love,
Mala

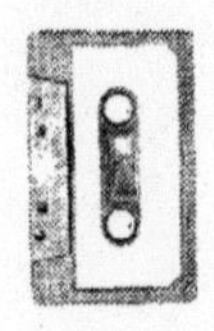

24 September

Hi, Shane! I'm lying in the hide right now and I can talk as the parent birds are out feeding. The three eggs still haven't hatched, but it shouldn't be long. I've just got to get photos of the chicks to bring the project full circle, which means I should be finished within a week. It's looking pretty good to me, especially the series I've got on the parents' mating. If all goes well, I'll be sending you the negatives and article next week – fingers crossed you like them.

You know how I've been looking for a new slant on my next project, rather than just doing straight description of behaviour and environment? Well, something's come up that has greater social implications, and I think it could be really worthwhile. Anyway, here it is – tell me what you think.

There's a myth in Esperance that's been around for years, apparently going back as far as the arrival of the first Europeans. The locals think there's a huge bird, big enough to carry away adult humans, living in the region. Did you see in the news a few weeks back, a hang-glider crashed into the sea east of here? Well, the rumour in town is that this giant bird attacked him.

How about if *Rare Earth*, through me, took part in the debate by offering a scientific point of view? After all, science is supposed to be about understanding what *is*. We do all kinds of studies explaining and exposing life on this planet, why not a systematic search for this mythical bird? NASA has a project to silence those crazy claims of UFO sightings once and for all. They've got a team scanning our solar system, searching for any signs of communication from other planets or alien spacecraft.

Don't forget, Shane, I've known what it's like to be ruled by ignorance and superstition. My parents didn't leave India only to get away from the pollution and overcrowding, but also so their children would be able to grow up without all the superstition. Like in my mother's village, where the local Sadhu or holy man would sit for hours meditating in the sun during the hottest part of the day and with four bonfires around him. It's a practice called 'Panchagni Tapas', which means 'five fires'. Now what sort of wisdom could you possibly get from that?

And my grandmother, she's a sweet old thing, but her whole life is ruled by superstition and she won't make a decision without consulting her astrologer. She's got a little altar by her bed, with a gaudy picture, like something you would find at a fair, of an eagle carrying two people. The eagle is called Garuda and the couple are Vishnu and Lakshmi. Vishnu has dark blue skin, and he's holding a mace, a sea-shell, a disc and a lotus-flower in each hand – yes, Shane, four arms. This trio is supposed to represent the gods of continued existence. My grandmother believes in that picture literally, that these gods fly around supporting Life. If I told her that a giant eagle had killed someone, she wouldn't believe me. 'Oh Mala,' she'd say, 'not Garuda. Garuda brings life. Watch out for Siva. It's Siva who destroys.'

I think it's a terrible shame that her life is ruled by such nonsense, and that kind of ignorance has no place in this country either. If we present the scientific facts about this so-called giant bird, we can put a stop to one superstition, at least.

Anyway, several people down here claim to have seen a bird bigger than any other. But how big do they mean? Does it weigh half a ton, like the flightless elephant bird did in Madagascar? Or is it like the condor, with a wing-span of three metres? There was a raptor that lived fifteen to twenty million years ago in Argentina, called an 'Argentavis', which had a six-metre wing-span. Our biggest raptor is the wedge-tailed eagle, and its wing-span is only two-and-a-half metres. There are a hundred other questions, like how could it have survived all this time without greater detection? Will it survive much longer, or will it have to rely on human aid for its future survival, like the Californian condor?

For the sake of the argument, what if the bird really

does exist and I find it? That would create a sensation and it would be your magazine that would bring it to the world!

In all this mishmash of speculation, there is one fact. All the reported sightings are east of here, that is, east of Esperance.

What I'd like to do is take a four-week trip to visit the places where the bird is supposed to have been seen. If this bird exists, it would surely leave some kind of trail somewhere, somehow. And when I don't find the bird, or any evidence of its existence, I'll do a piece covering the sites and say how occurrences such as the hang-glider accident, where something remains unexplained, allow the myth to thrive. What do you think?

I've asked Greg Muir to come with me. Do you remember him – he's the one I almost married. As you know, I chose to marry my work instead! He runs a raptor sanctuary now at Deep River. But don't get the wrong idea, Shane, I'm not giving in and becoming the helpless female having to rely on a man. He's an experienced bushman and knows about the desert. Also, I could use his muscle and his gear, like a boat and winches. Common sense tells me it's too risky to go so far off the beaten track by myself. I did wonder if I was doing the right thing by inviting him, though . . .

Well, that's it for now. I'm looking forward to hearing your reaction. I've still got a stack of tapes, so I'll keep sending them to you – that's if you agree, of course! Love from me, Mala

P.S. This is later – I'm back in my cottage now. Greg just phoned to say he's bringing a sixteen-year-old kid with him. What's your French like, Shane? Doesn't 'esperance' mean hope?

Every day of that first week, either Graham or Burwood drove Simon from his hostel to the sanctuary. Sometimes he worked only in the afternoons; sometimes he spent the entire day there. At dusk he would meet Muir at the sanctuary office, attached to the house, and be taken back. The routine was a simple one, but in everything he saw about the place – every task he was asked to do – he felt threatened. Still, he had not run as expected.

On days when he had a gap in his duties, Simon watched Muir working with the birds. There were two in particular, both black kites, one called Koko, the other Johnny, which the man was most concerned with. Once, when he thought his presence went unnoticed, the boy had seen Muir treating their injuries. They had been caught in rabbit traps and the man tended to their wounds seated on the floor of their huge aviary. He caught them up carefully, using both hands, crooning to them and soothing them with soft words, then he settled them between his thighs and massaged their injured legs, each stroke of his fingers firm yet gentle.

At other times the boy sat in the back row of a small public viewing stand, trying to appear invisible, while Muir worked. He would take the birds from their aviaries, put them in a carry-cage and release them in the sanctuary's 'free fly' area. Once freed, the birds would fly off to perch on a high branch nearby. There they would stretch their wings with a flap or two, moving from one foot to another, and scrape their beaks against the bark. Then they would take to the air again, gliding, circling, soaring.

Simon envied them. Still, they did not fly free for long. If Muir called their names they would circle and swoop down for the pieces of meat that he tossed to them. The boy hated to see their freedom cut short – especially at the call of a man; especially to be fed by him, to be dependent on him. Though Simon knew this was what had to be, since the birds had been injured and were growing stronger every day. He promised himself that he would never be the same, that he would never let this man, let any man, trap him and cage him. Never let anyone limit his freedom.

In the second week Simon reached his breaking point. Muir asked him to clean the toilets.

'The toilets?'

'The visitors' toilets.'

Simon turned in the direction Muir had pointed, then looked back, apparently confused. 'What's cleaning toilets got to do with me?'

'It's just helping out.'

'I have been, but no-one said anything about cleaning toilets.'

'Someone has to do it.'

'Why me?'

'Why not you?'

'You own the place. You do it.'

'I do sometimes. Everyone on staff takes a turn at jobs like that.'

'I bet they get paid for it.'

'Simon, you know that paying you wasn't part of the deal.'

'I've got friends on the dole. They get paid and they don't do anything.' He was starting to enjoy this game.

Muir took a deep breath. 'Look, how about you try being a bit positive. Try telling yourself that you might learn something here. Something worthwhile.'

'Like what? How to pick cigarette butts out of a urinal?' He was feeling pleased with himself. Scoring well.

'OK. What *were* you expecting to do today?'

'Not clean toilets, that's for sure.'

'Tell me, when you were driven down this morning, what did you think you'd be doing?'

'I didn't think about it.'

Muir sighed. 'Simon, I don't have time for this. How about you take a walk. If you see one of the staff who's doing something that looks interesting, something that takes your fancy, you might think about giving them a hand. OK?'

But the boy had no intention of giving anyone a hand.

For a time he tagged along behind a tour group, half-listening to the commentary. He presented himself for lunch at the sanctuary canteen, ate a hamburger and drank a milk shake alone, then disappeared among the tangle of shrubbery and pathways. Late that afternoon, when it was hot, he took a nap on the bench he had discovered by the dead-end path at the far end of the sanctuary. At dusk he woke to the haunting yelp of the lone, caged eagle. Long shadows were falling, and the gathering darkness unnerved him. He hurried back to Muir's office, eager to get out of the place.

Every other day Muir had been at his desk, busy with paperwork, but this time the room was empty and the boy slumped in a chair to wait. In front of him was a coffee table stacked with nature magazines. He picked one up and flicked through it, then dropped it back on the pile. He was no reader. He glanced around: a grey metal filing cabinet, a set of pine book shelves filled with dog-eared books on birds, a desk stacked with papers. Nothing that interested him – that 'took his fancy' as Muir had put it. But behind the desk, pinned up on a wall-mounted noticeboard, he saw a group of photographs. There were six or eight, each of an eagle soaring, all arranged around one central image: a shot of a gigantic nest of sticks and branches that cradled a single egg.

The boy had spent time in a photographic studio once, and recognised quality photographs when he saw them.

He noticed that between the prints, pinned in no particular order, were half a dozen newspaper clippings – or photocopies of newspaper clippings – each very small and yellowed with age. There was something about the arrangement of these images that attracted him, that led him across the room and around the desk to stand before them. He looked at them, his head cocked to one side – as was his way – to focus his single eye.

'You like those photos?' Muir asked from behind him.

Simon avoided the question. 'Who took them?' he said.

'Her name's Mala. Mala Glass . . .'

'What sort of a name's that?'

'Mala? It means "a circle or garland of flowers". Her father's European, her mother's Indian. They migrated to Australia when she was a girl. She's an amazing woman, Mala. A photojournalist. A real professional. Does photo essays for natural science and environmental magazines, mostly.' As he spoke, there was the trace of a smile on Muir's face.

The boy noticed. 'She your girlfriend?'

'She was once. Sort of. Before I came down here to start this place. We did biology together at uni. Both majored in ornithology. The study of birds. I liked her a lot, but that was six or seven years ago . . . and life got in the way, I guess . . .' He started stacking a pile of magazines.

Simon turned to face him. 'What do you mean, "Life got in the way"?'

'After graduation I took a job with the Conservation Council for a couple of years, then I opened this place. I always hoped that Mala would work here with me, you know, be with me, but she wanted to go on with her studies, and her photography . . .' He nodded towards the photos. 'She's doing a higher degree now, a doctorate on an endangered parrot, would you believe, but she still has time to do freelance photography. And write. Gets plenty of her work published too. She's always got photos in some magazine. Anyway, that's how it is. Like I said, life got in the way.'

'Do you ever see her?'

'She travels a fair bit but I usually know where she is.' Muir stopped talking and the boy looked at him, waiting for him to go on. 'She's the reason that you're at the sanctuary, in some ways. I often have the Youth Endeavour Progamme boys working down here, you see, but when I told Graham and Burwood that I was thinking of going bush on this research expedition with her, they asked if I could take you along. I said OK, but it depended on you. How you worked out. I thought that you might like being on the move every day, out in the open . . . since you used to be a runner, see?'

Simon pretended not to have heard and looked back at the photographs. The shots were good. The localities wild. Adventurous. It occurred to him that he would like to meet this Mala Glass. That he might like her. Although he probably wouldn't, if she was dumb and ugly enough to like Muir. 'What's so special about these old clippings?' he said, side-tracking. 'How come they're stuck up here?'

Muir rattled the car keys. 'I have to get you back to the hostel or you'll be late for dinner. I can tell you on the way, if you like.'

But once he was in the car, the boy slipped into one of his moods. Not once did he turn his face from the dark beyond the window, and the subjects of the photographs and the trek with Mala Glass were lost in the long silence of the drive.

3 October

Hello Shane. Great to get your letter – I'm glad to hear you've settled back in at work.

It's fantastic that you're interested in the new project! Don't worry about the cash advance by the way, I didn't really think I'd get it, but I'm sure the story will make a great spread. I've already started hunting around for background information on the Big Bird and last week I had some rather interesting conversations.

I went to have a talk with the Esperance police, since they had investigated the hang-glider's disappearance. Their station is no different from any you might walk into in this country – grey linoleum floors, long front counter, standard issue wooden desks. Why do they decorate the walls with those lifeless portraits of the missing or escaped? Great taste.

The first cop I spoke to must have just graduated, he looked so wet behind the ears and he was so earnest. Very cute. But he didn't seem to know much and he was clearly not sure how much he was allowed to tell me. The sergeant soon poked his head out of his office to see who was asking all the questions, and when he saw me he came over to find out what I wanted. He was out to impress, to show that he knew everything, since he was the officer in charge of the investigation. I wasn't going to let his interest in me and the stench of cigarettes on his breath stop me from getting the information.

Well, Shane, I don't think you'll be surprised to learn that, unlike what you see on TV, when the police mount a rescue here, they don't just jump into their helicopters and swing into action. They have to drive, and that can take hours, if not days. It's a small station, so for an emergency like this hang-glider accident they recruited some local abalone divers to help out.

The sergeant said they'd located the site of the crash but, even after three days of searching, they'd found no trace of the craft or pilot. They reckon that after hitting the cliff it slid straight into the water. Apparently the currents and swell in that area are exceptionally strong, so the search was difficult and dangerous. The sergeant said the wreckage must have been swept away in the time it took for them to arrive and he expects it to be found washed up on one of the beaches later. He reckoned that the body was more likely to have been food for the white pointer sharks that cruise the base of the cliffs than for a bird, no matter how big. With a little female know-how, I managed to get a copy of the hang-glider pilot's statement. I'm sure it was totally illegal for them to part with it, and they could probably lose their jobs, but they gave it to me.

The sergeant was much more interested in another theory. Apparently the two hang-gliders had passed through Esperance on their way east and had been in the pub, drinking. Their big talk about their travels around Australia must have impressed one of the local girls because, according to the witnesses, she was flirting with both of them. The old sergeant got very excited when he was telling me how she was cuddling up to the surviving pilot in his distress (or, as the sergeant believes, mock distress). His theory is that one of the hang-gliders became jealous about this girl and sabotaged his friend's glider to make him crash, but he's got no evidence to base it on. According to the sergeant, 'the only bird involved in this case wears a skirt'.

He also said a few harsh words about such guys and their heroics, going off into remote places to play then, when things go wrong, expecting immediate help at the taxpayer's expense. But hearing him describe his part in the search, and how well he led the little team, I'm sure he also had a great time playing the hero.

He really was a sleaze. I was bending over the table looking at the maps he had spread out, and as he was showing me the co-ordinates of the crash site he leant right in close to me. Once he was next to my ear he started saying things like, 'It's dangerous for a nice young girl like you to be going out there alone.' He reckoned that I should wait for a couple of weeks until he could get some time off work to take me and show me around. Dream on. What journalists have to do to get to the bottom of a story!

That's it for now, Shane, talk to you again soon.

Cheers.

The day after the toilet cleaning episode, Simon was dropped off late in the afternoon. Muir was waiting for him outside his office. 'So,' he said, meeting him with a wide smile, 'Feeling a bit more positive today?'

'I'm OK.' The boy was always wary of wide smiles.

Muir's expression became serious. 'Look Simon,' he said, 'I had a think about yesterday. You know, that cleaning job I asked you to do. I guess I was out of line . . . All right?'

Simon nodded vaguely. He was uncertain where this conversation was heading and figured it was best to remain non-committal.

'I was wondering if you'd like to have a go at something a bit more responsible today. A bit more interesting.'

'Such as?'

Muir led him to a tin shed at the back of the house. He opened it and went in. It was dark inside and the boy hovered at the door. Through the gloom he made out three old refrigerators standing in a row against the far wall, then he backed away. Something really stank in there. Something dead. He covered his face. 'Phew,' he muttered. 'What stinks?'

'You get used to it.' Muir groped in the darkness then dragged a heavy-duty plastic bag to the door and opened it towards the light. 'Take a look.'

The stench was almost more than the boy could bear. He felt his stomach turn, but leaned forward to see. Inside the bag was the body of an animal. 'What is it?' he asked.

'Move back from the door,' Muir said. 'I have to bring it out' When he was through, he opened the bag again. 'It's a dead 'roo. Road kill, I'm sorry to say. If one of the staff spots the carcass of an animal by the road, they'll bring it in. If it's too big I might take the ute out and collect it myself. We use it to feed the birds. Saves money and keeps the highways clean. Pretty hard on the nose, though, but the birds like a bit of rancid flesh. Rabbits and possums are OK as they are, but the trouble is, a fair-size 'roo like this one has to be cut up. Sawn into pieces, you know, before it can be distributed . . .'

Simon prepared for what was coming. Yesterday the lavatories, today hacking up road kill. 'I'm not doing that,' he said. 'I'm not cutting that up.'

Muir laughed. 'I wasn't expecting you to. I'll do it myself – there's an art to it. But I did want you to do some feeding. That's why I asked that you be brought over later today. We usually feed the birds from mid-afternoon until dusk. Just wait a minute . . .' He went back into the shed. A refrigerator door was opened, then closed. When he returned he was holding a carton. He put it on the ground at the boy's feet and folded back the cardboard flaps. Inside were the bodies of white rats, laid side by side like sausages in a butcher's window. 'The smaller birds eat these. We get them from the university. They breed them there for experiments, or places like this. Herpetologists take a few.'

The boy shook his head, not understanding.

'People who keep snakes. There's more of them around than you'd think.'

'So you want me to feed these to the birds?'

'I do. Yes.'

'But only the small birds?'

'I'll show you which ones. Owls. Frogmouths. Some of the hawks.'

'And if I do it, I don't have to go in the cage, or anything?'

'No. You just open the door and chuck the carcass in. No more than one rat to a bird . . . You're not worried about this are you? You know, scared of the birds?'

'Why should I be scared?' He knew very well that he had answered one question with another, which was no answer at all.

'A lot of people are.'

'I only do what I want.' He knew that this was not true either. He knew that there were many things that he did without wanting to. At least, without having respect for himself when he had done them.

'So,' Muir said, taking his reply as affirmation, 'you'll do it?'

'I guess so. If you show me how. And where to start.'

Muir picked up the carton and headed towards the cages. Simon followed, wondering why in the world he was doing this. Why he hadn't left this place on the first day. Or the second. Yet here he was still, on the fifth day. And following this man. Actually *following* him. What was going on here? What was wrong with him?

'The cages either side of the path here house the small raptors,' Muir explained. 'They're the birds that will take these rats. I'll show you what to do, and after that you're on your own. The main thing is not to overfeed them. They'll eat just about anything that's thrown to them, but since they don't exercise enough, stuck in these cages, they can get sluggish. Just watch what I do and do the same. One rodent per bird. That's all it takes. No more. No less. OK?'

He went to the first cage and looked in. 'One grey falcon in here,' he said. 'One rat.' He reached into the carton and picked up a carcass. He took some keys from his belt and unlocked the door, opening it just wide enough to toss the carcass inside, then shut and locked it again.

Hardly had he stood up when a pale shadow fell from beneath the roof. It was so fast that Simon couldn't follow it and would have remained uncertain of having seen it at all, except that no sooner had it fallen than the carcass of the rat Muir had thrown down was gone. Though not gone exactly. It suddenly appeared – in the blink of an eye – as a limp, white shape against the darkness high in the cage.

'See that?' Muir said. 'She swooped down, picked it up and took it back to her perch before you even knew. Believe me, you have to watch them.'

'I thought they were too hurt to fly.'

'Some are. Depends on the nature of their injury. Some were poisoned by toxic sprays. Some have crippled feet from traps. Some have lost an eye . . .' The man realised his blunder and was silent, but Simon said nothing.

When Muir had given two more demonstrations, he told the boy to try the next cage himself. He would watch. Simon picked up the carton, carried it along the path and put it down outside the cage. He checked the number of birds – there were three – and removed that number of carcasses from the carton. Next he took the keys from Muir, checked that he had the correct one and unlocked the cage. As he had been told, he was careful not to open the door until he was certain that the birds were well clear and that he had the carcasses at hand. Satisfied that he had taken all precautions, and aware that he was being watched, he opened the door and threw the carcasses in. Seconds later the door was closed, the lock secured and he stood back.

'Great stuff,' Muir said. 'I'll leave you to it. There's this row, and the next. Mostly harriers, falcons and hawks. A few kites. Take your time. And try to enjoy yourself. See you back at the office.'

Simon was not convinced that he would enjoy himself, nor did he need to be told to take his time. He had already decided to do that. Why should he hurry? When he had finished he would only be given another job. Or be taken back to the hostel.

Once Muir was out of sight Simon dragged the box of rats off the path into the shade and sat down. For some time he watched the three birds he had fed. The sign on the cage said that they were harriers and he remembered that there were jets or rockets with nuclear warheads called that. One of the three had taken a rat back up to its perch. The bird kept one foot on it, but was not eating. The other two were on the ground. Each had taken a rat and was dismembering it. They were not big birds, hardly more than a pigeon in size, but very strong. They tore at the soft white fur, keeping one taloned foot on their prey to steady it as they ate – or maybe to convince themselves that they had caught it, that it was still alive and might escape.

He noticed that every so often one of the pair made an attempt to fly; to take the carcass up to a perch. But one wing drooped lower than the other and he realised that this was the bird's reason for being there. He examined the others, looking for tell-tale signs of their injuries, but could see nothing.

He turned his attention to the bodies of the white rats beside him. The box was open and the soft afternoon light dappled their skins pale blue and green and grey. He glanced again at the birds as they fed. The carcasses they tore at were no longer white, but splattered with blood, the flesh exposed, shiny and red. The rest was no more than guts, some blue, some black. He looked back at the rats in the box and stroked one gently. He was struck by its softness and pressed harder. He brought two fingertips together, pinching the fur and pulling up, tugging at it as the birds had done. It lifted a little before he felt any tension; before he felt it tighten to form a pyramid of taut fur. When he pulled harder the body itself lifted, separating from those that lay beside it. He brought his other hand down and cupped the creature in his palm. He raised it to his face, examining the tiny claws of the front feet, the nipples on the pink-skinned stomach, the teeth that protruded over the thin grey lips. He lifted it higher until it almost touched his nose. He smelt it and was surprised by its sweetness – like the smell of a new baby – then, as he drew it away from himself, he saw the pink eyes and wondered at their last sight, at that last bright moment before the blind dark of death. In one eye, at least, he knew that dark.

He replaced the rat, surprising himself that he troubled to curl the tail around the body so that all was in order, and then he settled himself back on his elbows.

For a time he enjoyed the last warmth of the sun, but he felt the restlessness beginning to grow, the uneasy churning that began in his stomach then spread through his body, telling him that it was time to go. That he had finished with this place.

Yet Muir had not been hard on him. The man was not a fool, like so many others who had tried to take him in hand. He had given him some space. And the night before, as he had talked about the photographs and his girlfriend, the photographer, he had seemed OK. Still, there was the beginning of the urge to go. To run. The usual tell-tale tightness. The unease. But for now he would do as he had been asked – for now it suited him – so he picked up the carton and stepped onto the path.

When he had tended five cages he stopped and looked back. At each cage he had carefully followed the routine that Muir had established. He thought about this. That he had taken the trouble vaguely unsettled him, left him strangely unfamiliar with himself.

Still, he went on. The next cage was marked 'sparrow-hawk'. Following the routine, he put down the carton and peered in. High up he saw a single bird: an insignificant, sad-looking thing, its drab brown feathers askew. It sat very still, its eyes dull and half-closed. He ran his fingers across the cage wire, making it hum, but the bird paid him no attention. He whistled at it and made clucking sounds in the back of his throat, but the bird neither turned nor looked down. He laughed at his own foolishness. What difference did it make to him if the stupid thing sat there forever?

He took a rat from the box and put it on the ground beside the cage door. He selected the correct key from those that Muir had left him, inserted it in the lock, released it, picked up the carcass and opened the door. In that instant he felt a rush of air like a sudden wind and something brushed his cheek. Instinctively he slammed the door shut. He raised one hand to touch his face, but even as he did he guessed what had happened. There had been a second bird. A second sparrow-hawk in this cage that he had failed to see. It had been on the floor of the aviary, to his left, as he knelt to open the door. That was his blind spot. That half of the world which he could not see. Which he honestly could not see.

He tossed aside the limp white body in his hand and sprang to his feet. In the moment of regret that he allowed himself he kicked the carton aside, spilling its contents onto the path.

Then he ran.

The police found Simon at a bus station later that night. It was almost as if he were waiting to be found – the place was so public, so obvious, and so brightly lit. At noon the next day, accompanied by Burwood, he was returned to the Deep River Sanctuary. He waited in the car while the counsellor went in to Muir's office and then he was asked to come in himself. Muir was at his desk, waiting for him, and Burwood left them together.

'I think we should take a walk,' Muir suggested, getting up. 'There's a few things we have to straighten out, wouldn't you say?'

Simon did not answer, although he followed, as asked.

For some time they said nothing, doing no more than wandering through the sanctuary paths, keeping their distance. From time to time Muir glanced across, hoping to read something in the boy's expression that would allow him to speak, but he saw nothing. Simon held his head high and seemed relaxed enough, although he constantly ran his fingers through his hair, drawing it forward to cover his dead eye.

Finally Muir said, 'It's time we talked, don't you think?'

The boy looked down at the path. 'I'm listening,' he answered.

'First up, I just want to ask you a couple of questions. Like, how that bird got out. That sparrow-hawk.'

'I didn't see it. I stuffed up. That's all.'

'OK. Fair enough. I just wanted to know. We caught it down by the sanctuary fence, by the way. Some kid had filled it with lead from a slug gun, so it couldn't have flown far. But I just wanted to know . . .'

'It flew pretty fast when it got past me. That's what happened. It got out when I opened the cage door.'

'I warned you to watch out for that. I said to take a good look before you opened up. I told you to . . .'

Simon stopped. 'Here,' he said, 'take a good look at me. At my eyes. See?' he pulled back the hair that fell across his forehead. 'See? I've got one eye? This one's glass, just in case you hadn't noticed. Sometimes I miss things. Like that bird. It was right down at the left of the cage and when I opened the door, it took off. Just like that' He clicked his fingers. 'It was an accident. OK? An accident.' With that, he walked on ahead.

'It doesn't matter,' Muir called, his long strides closing the gap. 'We found the bird. That's what matters.'

Simon laughed. 'No it's not. What matters is that I got it wrong. That's the first thing you wanted to say, isn't it? And that's how come I ran – that's the next question you're going to ask, isn't it. Isn't it?'

Muir had slowed his pace, and now stopped. 'You're right,' he said. 'Since it's my place that you ran away from, and my bird that you let go, my rats that you left to the flies and the ants, and my trust that you betrayed – I'd say I've got every right to want to know.'

Muir moved closer, to face him. 'Look,' he said, 'forget all about yesterday. It's old news. I've got a proposition to put to you, and I'm asking you to think about it, all right?'

Simon shrugged. 'Don't have much choice, do I?'

'Yes, you've got a choice. You can go back to the hostel right now, if you want. I'll take you myself.'

The boy said nothing.

'OK, here goes. The other night when you were in my office we were talking about those photos of the eagles that Mala Glass took. You remember? And you asked me about the press clippings that were pinned up next to them . . .'

'Yes.'

'Well, it's those clippings I want to talk about. You see, for over a hundred years there've been rumours that a giant bird lives somewhere to the south of here, southeast, really, somewhere near Esperance. Sometimes nothing's heard about it for twenty years or so, and then, out of the blue, a story turns up. Another sighting. OK? With her background in both ornithology and photojournalism,

Mala's been keen to do a story on the big bird ever since she started going down to Esperance years ago. Mala's what you would call a "stickler for the truth", I guess. Well, last month she sent me a clipping of a newspaper story about a hang-glider pilot who was supposed to have been knocked out of the sky and killed by a huge bird. An eagle, maybe. As usual, the authorities dismissed the whole thing. Unreliable witnesses. Lack of evidence. It's always the same. A hoax, like the Yeti. Or the Loch Ness Monster. But if you stand back a bit and look at the historical evidence, instead of treating each sighting as nothing but a sensational page filler in the Sunday papers, there could be a giant bird down there. I mean, every witness can't be lying. There has to be something there. There just has to be . . .

'I was going to tell you this in the car the other night, but you didn't seem too interested, so I let it go. But Mala's been planning this trek – the one mentioned on your first day – to try to get to the bottom of these big bird rumours once and for all. She asked me to go with her. When I told Graham and Burwood, they suggested it might be an idea to take you, if you were willing to come. I wasn't so sure if it was a good idea at first, what with me and Mala, and the way things were, but then I thought it might work, ease the tension, so to speak, so I'm asking you to come. Pain in the bum that you are. OK?'

Simon was taken aback. The man's honesty had caught him off guard, and he looked away, embarrassed.

Muir took the chance to catch his second wind. 'Look,

Simon, whatever you decide it's all the same to me. But be warned. If you come, it's going to be tough. Three or four weeks in the bush. No luxuries. And here's the really hard part. As you said, or predicted, on your first day, Graham and Burwood will only supply your gear – a backpack, some camping equipment, bed roll – that sort of thing – if I write a report on your . . . well . . . your behaviour. Your attitude – I'm not sure of the word – when we get back . . .'

The boy nodded. He had been listening. 'So how far is this place?' he asked.

'Esperance? About a thousand k's from here. But I can't prove that's where the bird is. That's just the nearest town to where it's been sighted. It could be hundreds of k's from there. Further to the south there are islands, so I'll take the run-about. Or it could be to the north, in the desert. I don't know. That's what we're going for. To find out.'

They were nearing the end of the path and Muir stopped to sit on the bench by the cage of the lone eagle.

'How long will it take, did you say?'

'I don't know. A couple of days just to reach Esperance. And then we'll have to walk. Backpack. I'd say maybe three weeks, all up. I couldn't leave the sanctuary for any longer. Not to the day staff.'

'And we'd be alone, just the three of us, out in the bush?'

'I'd be very surprised if we weren't.'

Finally the boy said, 'Why not? Sure, I'll come.' But he kept his reasons to himself, which had always been his way.

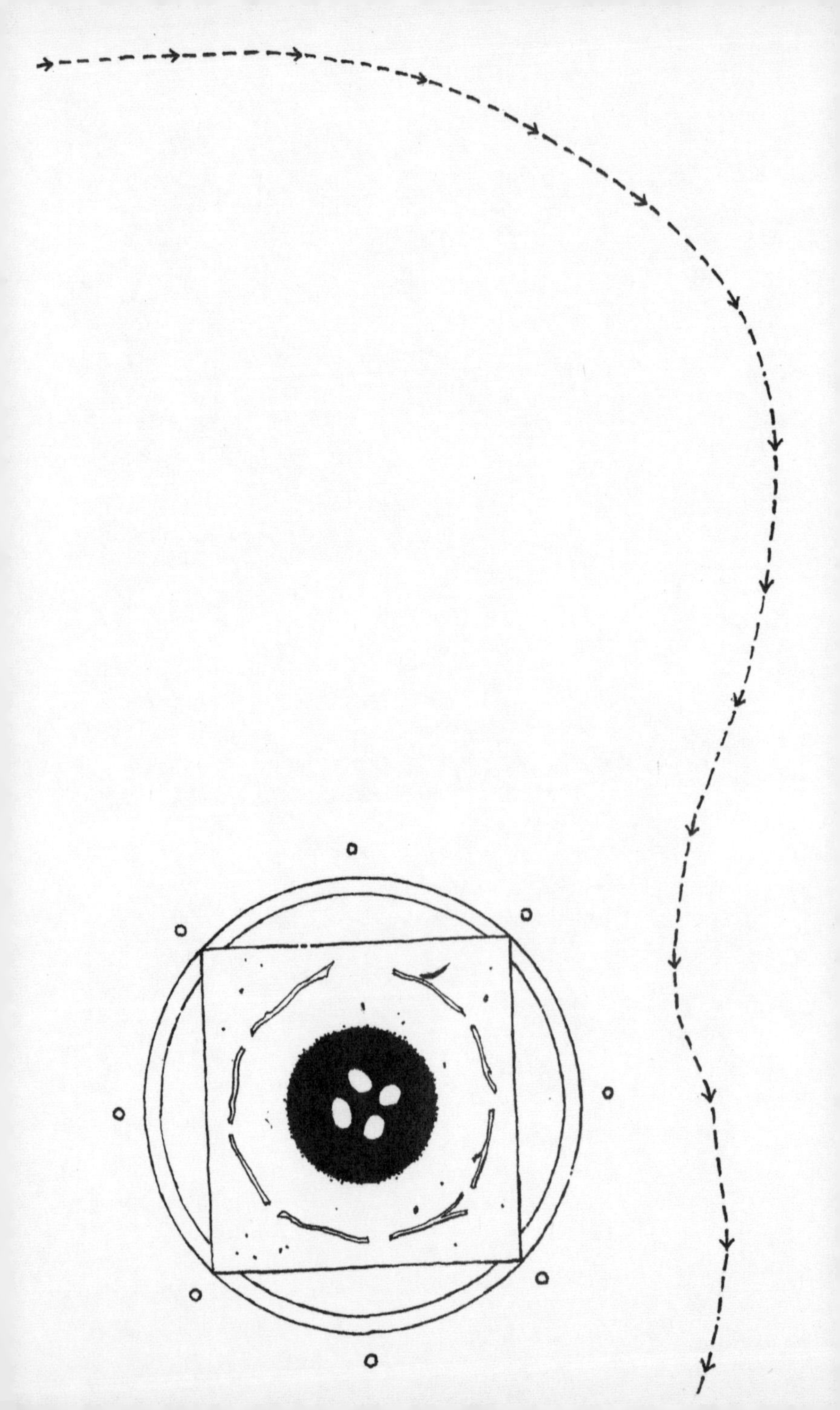

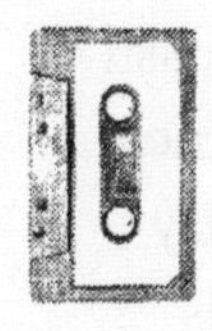

5 October

Shane, hi! I've got good news for you. All three ground-parrot eggs have hatched and as far as I can tell they're doing fine – so the article is on the way.

About the giant bird story – the more I talk about it down here, the more I realise how widespread the belief is. The local National Park ranger's a friend of mine and he suggested that if I wanted to learn a thing or two about the myth of the bird I should visit the Esperance museum. So last Thursday I went across to see what I could find. You'll see from the photographs that it's right on the main street in a converted railway siding. It's a great cavernous shed with a corrugated iron shell around a forest of huge wooden pillars and beams. I could only get exterior shots as no cameras were allowed inside. The women in the formal group pose (they wouldn't have it any other way) are the volunteers who run the placc. Walking inside reminded me of India, somewhere like Varanasi, where you see millions of pilgrims all vying for a precious space on the ghats of the Ganges. Everywhere I looked, every inch of space, was filled with debris from the past. And like the devotees of Varanasi, I guess, each piece could tell a story.

The first display I saw was a glass cabinet of fossil bones and teeth from local dinosaurs, none of which were birds. Next to that was a photographic display of rare and endangered flora and fauna. The walls were covered in sepia photographs showing explorers, standing proud, ready to set out with their Aboriginal guides and loaded camels. I read that after Burke and Wills first brought out twenty-four camels from Peshawar to Australia for their expedition in 1860, camels were then used extensively as pack animals across the outback. Sealers' clubs and whalers' harpoons lay across the rung of a dinghy whose wood had been softened by wear and age. Next to it was the wreckage of a schooner, and suspended from the rafters were pieces of the Skylab that broke up over here, showering Esperance with space junk like falling stars.

Shane, as I looked at this display I couldn't help thinking how, in all our attempts to conquer the world, every scheme has fallen victim to the powers of nature. It's ironic that these glass cabinets and the tourist dollar are the current defences against the ravages of time and change.

I was curious to meet the people who look after this place, to see what they might know about the big bird. I could hear a great deal of laughing and chatter behind a door marked 'Staff Only'. I knocked and entered, and as I did the people in the room fell silent. There were eight or so women all scrunched in around a table that was littered with papers, knitting and balls of wool, bottles of polish and rags. All eyes were turned inquiringly towards me.

A tall, straight-backed woman introduced herself and asked what I wanted. I told them I was interested in finding out about the 'giant' bird, but her face stayed stiff, not a muscle moved, not even to blink, as if she was suspicious of me. It was only when I explained how serious I was in my research into the bird's existence that she smiled – a warm smile – and said, 'I'm sure these ladies will be able to help.'

They invited me to join them at the table and excitedly pushed up to make room. Think of it, Shane, these women, with their sagging skin barely covering their frail bones, with perms to put shape back into their grey hair, they're the new leaders in fighting the effects of time. I couldn't help thinking it's a pity there aren't more young people interested in preserving their history.

Before I was allowed to ask any questions, the women insisted on making me a cup of tea. It was such a performance – the fine china cups and all – the precision of the preparation reminded me of an Oriental ceremony. The moment I was handed my tea they started. One tiny lady with a thin voice said, 'Now dear, you don't want to meddle with that bird. It's bad luck.' She went on to say that the old sealers who lived among the islands called it the 'Wazo' and told stories of seeing it mainly in 'the bad years'. They also believed that it came up from the depths of the ocean, rising with the sun. When she'd finished the other women laughed, and gently scolded her for trying to scare me.

Shane, I've just realised why they call this mythical bird the 'Wazo'. It must be an Australianised version of *oiseau*, the French for 'bird'!

Dot – I think that was her name – then started telling stories she had heard from the prospectors up north. She said, 'In the bad years the Wazo was like a ghost, almost invisible, hovering in the sky, ready to pounce on the dying.'

The tall woman who had first greeted me accused them of being a morbid lot. She said what I wanted were facts, not just old men's ghost stories. Then she gave me that stare again and said that I should speak to Dr Gwen, a woman who had actually seen the bird when she was a child. She promptly ordered one of the others to phone Gwen to get her to come over.

As we waited, the rest of the women told me what they knew about the bird. One of them, who seemed to be made up of circles, with huge breasts, moon face and curly hair, mentioned Martin Abrahams. I'd read about him – he was a botanist back in 1873 and was the first to survey and catalogue the area.

They all talked at once, each convinced that she knew the facts, but they all had different versions.

They argued about when Abrahams was supposed to have been in the area, whether he was related to the Governor of the time, what he did, whether he was studying birds or plants – one of them said he was an 'orthinologist'. But they all agreed about what he found. According to them, it was an eggshell, at least 'two foot by three foot', maybe even more. They said he found it about 200 to 250 kilometres to the north.

But then one of them said, 'No, more north-east of here.'

'Yes, that's right dear, out near the telegraph station, out Eucla way.'

More recendy a couple of tourists claimed to have seen the Wazo. But even these women thought they were a bit crazy since the 'tourists' were out tracking UFOs when they saw the bird, 'over the hills to the east'. They couldn't name the hills but told me how to get there: 'When you're coming down from Norseman, before you get to where the road swerves west to avoid the salt pans, just there and to the east into the desert'.

I wonder how easy that's going to be to find!

After all this chatter there was a momentary lull, then the woman beside me spoke. She was in a bright floral dress, had red lips and sad, tired eyes. 'I've never mentioned this to anybody before,' she said, 'but my father told me that when he was a little boy, he and his family saw the Wazo when they were sailing back to

Esperance through the islands. They had to leave their land because they couldn't survive the long dries they have out east. The boat was just off Mondrain Island and he was lying on deck, having just woken, staring into the sky, when all of a sudden a bird the colour of water flew out from nowhere – the biggest, biggest bird he'd ever seen.' She said her father knew his birds and he swore it was the Wazo. She believed this wholeheartedly. She said she'd never known her father to lie.

This was all fine, but I wanted to get some facts – after all, that was the purpose of my visit – so I asked if they knew about the hang-glider who'd crashed at Hellfire Bay a month before. Well, you should have heard them! Some friend of a friend's daughter was a nurse on duty at the hospital when they brought in the hang-glider pilot. It was the day after the accident and the rescue party still couldn't find his mate. The nurse said the surviving pilot was hysterical. He was screaming that this giant bird had attacked his friend, grabbed the poor fellow in its claws and flown away. His description of the bird picking up the body was so gory – blood spurting out, spurting everywhere.

You can see I wasn't getting many facts from this tea party, but I couldn't leave as this woman, Dr Gwen, was coming in especially to speak to me. I drank my tea while the others continued telling their ghost stories and relating a myriad other strange happenings.

When the front door slammed they were suddenly quiet, almost as if in reverence. Someone whispered to me, 'That must be Gwen now. She's ninety-four, you know. She's the best doctor in the south. All her patients love her. You can't trust anyone these days, but the good doctor, ah, she stands alone.'

A small, sharp-featured woman walked in, her grey hair pulled back tight into a bun. She greeted everyone with a hearty, 'Morning, girls. How are we this morning?', sat down at the table and was barely introduced to me when she began telling me about herself. 'I'm ninety-four, you know,' she said. 'I've stayed healthy all my life. I just don't move as fast as I used to, that's all. Wouldn't change a day in my life.'

The second tape I've sent you is Dr Gwen's story. I'm keeping it for the details she gives, but I thought you might like to hear it and also get a sense of her character. You'll hear me interjecting occasionally and the other ladies are in the background – of course!

'So you want to know about the Wazo, do you? Well, let me tell you, I've seen it all right. Do you believe in it, or are you one of those 'experts' who says it doesn't exist?'

'Er . . . no . . . Dr Gwen. It's really good of you to come and talk to me, and help with my investigations. What I'm trying to do is track down solid evidence that will prove the existence of the Wazo. I'd love to hear what you know about it, if you don't mind.'

'I can only tell you what I saw. I was just a wee thing. Out fishing with my father.'

'Whereabouts?'

'If you would just hold your horses, girl, I'll tell you. Now, what was I saying? Yes, we'd gone out in our dinghy, but we'd landed on an island off Mississippi Point. We'd been out for days and managed to gather a large catch, mainly fish but also some seal. My father liked eating seal – he said it was good for your bones. Mind you, he'd make use of everything; nothing at all would be wasted.'

'Would you like some tea, Gwen?'

'Yes, dear, thank you. What was I saying? Oh yes, we were packing up camp when it happened. My father and I were making our way down the rock. Do you know those islands? They're mainly giant granite boulders, often round as a ball, so the sides get very steep. The granite is smooth, and if there's a bit of dew on the ground it's downright treacherous.

'We had our arms full, walking down this slope, when we heard a stillness, a strange silence. I'll remember that all the days of my life. The bird came from behind and hit my father. The force knocked him over but he scrambled back onto his feet to fight the thing off. He yelled to me, 'Get away, girl!' I felt the wind from its huge wings on my face as it swooped at us again. Those wings were as wide as, as . . . I don't know, as wide as that museum out there.'

'But that's about twenty metres!'

'Are you suggesting I'm lying, girl?'

'No. But that's huge, that's all.'

'I dropped everything and scampered across the rock into the low scrub. It was hardly any protection, but that's all there was, so I tried to bury myself in it. The next time it attacked my father he lost his footing and slid all the way to the bottom. I can still hear his scream.

'The Wazo was all bright, but not really a colour, more of a shimmering blue light, with yellow eyes. It landed on a rock opposite and I had time to get a good look at it. I wasn't game to come out, so I waited for what seemed an age until it flew away, swooping to grab a seal in its claws – not a pup, I'll have you know – an adult.

'I scrambled as fast as I could down to my father, all the time keeping an eye out in case it returned. I helped him from the water and sat with him on the rocks most of the day. He was never the same again.'

Well what do you think of that, Shane? All these women are convinced that this giant exists. It's scary what some people are willing to believe, isn't it? Surely Gwen's story is just a fantasy, but then there's something about that woman . . .

You should've seen how they fussed over me when I was leaving! I'd explained that I intended to go bush with a couple of friends to investigate the places they had talked about. They asked me to let them know how my search went, though I'm not sure they'll want to know me when I get back. They even presented me with a souvenir from the museum, a pocket-knife with a whale bone handle – very nice. Just as I was wondering what I was going to do with yet another knife, Gwen said something really odd – she said that when the time came I'd know who to give it to.

Anyway, that's it for now – talk to you soon.

Simon first saw Mala Glass through the window of Muir's car. It was just on dark when they drove up, and she was leaning on the verandah railing of her shack, staring out to sea. When she heard them she checked that it was Muir behind the wheel, then smiled and shook her head as if to say, 'Well, here we go again . . .'

She was better looking than the boy had expected. Tall, with short black hair – blue-black, he thought, and shining. Her skin was dark too, her cheek bones high and elegant, and he remembered that Muir had said that her parents came from India. This was clear to him now. She was beautiful, almost, but the simplicity of her dress – she wore shorts and army socks turned down over hiking boots – gave her an ordinariness that did not threaten him, though he was aware of the shape of her breasts beneath her white cotton shirt.

She approached the car on Muir's side, bending down to peer in. 'About time you got here,' she said. 'I was wondering how long you could get along without me.'

If Muir was supposed to reply he was given no opportunity. Before he could say a word she had reached in through the car window, offering to shake hands with the boy. 'Mala Glass,' she said. 'I guess you're Simon the Bad!'

He turned to take her extended hand, shaking it directly in front of Muir's face, forcing him to pull in his chin, his chest. 'Who said that I was bad?' he asked, and surprised himself by smiling back.

'A little bird,' she laughed and gave Muir a peck on the cheek.

'Hello, Mala,' was all Muir said.

She laughed again and moved back from the car as Muir got out. Simon did the same, stretching his long, cramped legs as he looked around. The shack was set in a grassy clearing overlooking the sea.

'That's the Great Southern Ocean,' Mala said, coming to stand beside him. 'Do you know what's on the other side of that?' She stood so close that he could smell her. Talcum powder. Or soap. A freshly showered smell.

'Antarctica,' he answered.

'That's right.' There was a hint of surprise in her voice. 'The great white continent. That would be the place to go, wouldn't it, if you were looking for adventure?'

He guessed that she was trying to draw him out, to lead him into conversation. Maybe she was trying to make up for her 'Simon the Bad' introduction. He didn't care. 'Be OK,' he said, 'if you were into that.' He put his hands in the pockets of his jeans and turned towards the shack. 'Is this place yours?'

She shook her head. 'Rented. The way I get about, travelling from job to job, there's no point in owning anything much, let alone a house. I've only got this for a few more weeks, until my assignment down here's finished. Pity in a way, I like it here. A lot.'

As she spoke he turned to look at her. She held her head

high and he noticed her long neck, the line of her jaw, her square chin and straight nose, the unblinking steadiness in her dark eyes. He turned away, afraid that he might be caught staring.

But she didn't seem to care if he was. 'Come on,' she said. 'We'd better give our Greg a hand unpacking the car or else we'll be in trouble. Then I'll see about something to eat.'

After dinner she and Muir sat on the verandah, drinking and talking about their plans for the search for the bird. Simon listened for a while, found the conversation boring and irrelevant to him – since he didn't really want to be there – then spread his sleeping bag on an old sofa in a corner of the shack and fell asleep, lulled by the sound of the sea.

He woke to the smell of bacon cooking. He pulled his jeans on, slipped outside to the bathroom annex, and went into the kitchen. Only Mala was there, breaking eggs over a frying pan. She was wearing shorts again. 'Morning,' she said. 'I thought the smell of this might wake you up.'

'Where's Greg?' he asked.

'I sent him in to Esperance to collect some supplies for the trip. He's been gone a good half hour. You were still in dreamland.'

The boy hated the thought of someone watching him while he slept, someone standing over him, staring down, laughing at him as he lay there with his mouth open, his stupid eye twitching.

'How come he went so early?'

Mala was too preoccupied with the food to answer. 'How many eggs?' she asked.

'Two,' he said, sitting down.

'You want toast?'

He nodded, expecting her to serve him, but she had no intention. 'You can make it. Toaster's right there. And the bread and butter.'

While he occupied himself with the toast, she answered his question. 'It's a good two hours' drive into town from here. And Greg's driving is pretty slow and steady, if I remember rightly. I'd say he won't be back until this afternoon.'

Simon laughed. 'I just drove a thousand k's with him – he never went over a hundred clicks all the way from the sanctuary. Boring, hey?'

She turned and gave him a strange look. 'You never can tell with Greg,' she said. 'Sometimes he's . . .' But she stopped herself and said instead, 'You ready to eat?'

She put his bacon and eggs on the table and he sat down. She perched on a high stool opposite, sipping coffee. There was a long silence.

When he had finished eating, he said, 'Can I have some coffee?'

'Sure, you can get it.'

He took a mug from the dresser and made the coffee, taking it black and sugarless, which he hated, but since that was how Mala was having hers he did the same. Then he stood by the window with his back to her and looked out over the shimmering blue of the morning sea.

'What were you thinking of doing with Greg away?' she asked.

'Nothing.'

'Nothing?'

'I didn't even know he was going out.'

'Well you don't have to hang around here like a bad smell, if that's what's worrying you. I could use you, if you want.'

'How do you mean?' In spite of the coffee, his mouth was dry, his voice thick.

She laughed, realising that he was just a boy, in spite of his height and build. 'I wasn't going to jump on you and have my way with you, if that's what you're thinking,' she said, laughing again. She pushed her chair back and stood up. 'Bring your coffee out onto the verandah and I'll tell you all about it.'

She sat in a weathered cane lounge and he leant against the railing, as he had first seen her the evening before. 'I'm not sure what Greg has told you about my work,' she said. 'I'm a photojournalist. That means I do freelance photographic assignments and I write the articles that go with them. Anyway, right now I'm finishing what we call a photo essay about an endangered parrot that lives around here. *Pezoporus wallicas.* The ground or swamp parrot, but I guess you're not into birds?'

He grinned and nodded. 'Not really.'

Too bad. They're not terribly attractive, as parrots go. They're a sort of dull, olive green with some yellow and black tips here and there. They're not very big either, no more than thirty centimetres from head to tail, but they're one of only three ground parrots species in the world and there aren't too many left. So I set up a contract with *Rare Earth* magazine to get them on film while they were still around. Since they're basically ground dwellers they're easy prey for introduced animals. Feral cats and foxes. And fires. And scrub clearing. It's a pity, but it's the same the world over. There are species endangered everywhere. And it's our fault. Humans, I mean . . .' She paused and sipped her coffee, possibly waiting for him to respond. He didn't, but she went on all the same.

'There's a pair of these parrots nesting not far from here, a kilometre or so along the beach at Mississippi Point. Only trouble is, the place is more of an island than a promontory. It's only connected to the beach by a causeway of rocks, and most of the time they're either under water or being belted by breakers, especially if the tide's in. Some fishermen had a length of cable strung across so they could get over – hand over hand, sort of thing – but that came away in a storm about a week ago, and with all my gear, I can't cross without it. I thought you might give me a hand down there, to get the cable up again. If you don't want to, that's OK.'

He shrugged. He hadn't been thinking of doing anything like this. In fact, since Muir was away it had seemed like a good time to shoot through. To run . . . Maybe she had suspected this. Maybe this was why she was asking, organising him. Keeping him trapped. Right there, under her nose.

But then she said, 'Don't worry. I'll go by myself. You can bum around here and when Greg comes back, tell him I'll be waiting for him down at Mississippi Point. I'll leave a mud-map. He'll find it. He's brilliant at things like that.'

Simon gave this some thought. There was something about her. Something alive. Adventurous. Free. 'No,' he finally muttered. 'I guess I could come. But, will we have to get wet. You know. Swim?' he asked.

She looked at him hard. 'No. Not swim, but you might get wet. Did you bring your bathers?'

'I've got shorts.'

'They'll do. If you want to come, that is.'

'I've got nothing else to do,' he said, surprising himself again.

'Great. Give me five minutes. That's all I need. What about you?'

'I'll have to get out of these jeans.'

'Have you got a pack?'

Simon shrugged. 'The counsellors gave me one at Deep River but I've got nothing to put in it.'

'A towel? Sunscreen? Water?'

'I've got a towel. But I'm not wearing any fancy sunscreen.'

'Well, you'll have to take water. I'll give you one of my canteens. I've got stacks.'

She left him to go into the shack, reappearing wearing her shorts over her bathers. In each hand she carried a black tote bag, obviously heavy, which he guessed was her camera equipment, and wedged beneath her arm was a water canteen. 'Here,' she said, putting down one of the bags, and holding out the canteen, 'I've filled this. Put it in your pack. And here's a present . . .'

In the palm of her hand lay a bone-handled pen knife. 'This old woman, Dr Gwen from the Esperance Museum, gave me this. I came across it in the bottom of my camera bag this morning. It sort of had your name on it, if you know what I mean.'

The boy gave her a quizzical look. 'Had my name on it?'

'It's just an expression. The bone, you know, it looked kind of tough, like you . . . Besides, a good knife always comes in handy when you're in the bush.'

'Thanks,' he said. 'Can I keep it?'

'Sure. Now, are we ready?'

When he nodded and tapped his thigh to show that he had changed into his shorts she gave a low, playful whistle at the sight of him. 'Nice legs,' she laughed, then stepped down off the verandah.

The morning was clear and hot and they walked together by the sea. Simon wore the backpack and carried one of the camera tote bags. Mala walked in the water, kicking up the last runners of the retreating waves. He stuck to the firm sand, moving away a little when an incoming wave crept up, threatening to wet him.

'Don't you like the water?' she finally asked.

'Not fussy,' he said.

'Not fussy? What do you mean, not fussy? I thought you'd be dying to dive in there.'

He shrugged. 'Never learnt to swim, did I?'

She slowed her pace. 'Really? How come?'

'Never met a Phys. Ed. teacher that I liked. All jerks they were, getting around in their red silk shorts. Always blowing their little silver whistles. Jump this. Hop that. Bend over . . .' It was the most that he had said, and when he realised he put his hand to his hair, pulling it down over his blind eye.

She noticed and changed the subject, talking cheerily about her work until they reached the end of the beach. 'This is it,' she said, pointing to a scrubby headland that stretched out into the sea. 'And there's the causeway. See where the waves are breaking?'

Simon shaded his eye, squinting into the sun. The distance between the beach and the headland was about twenty metres. The water was not deep – a metre, at most – but it was rough, crashing onto the chain of rocks in a welter of foam and spray and from this, momentarily, a single dripping rock would suddenly appear amongst a tangle of blood-red weed. He lowered his hand, saying nothing, although she guessed his concern.

'Are you game?' she asked.

'If you are.' But he had no real idea what he was supposed to be 'game' for. What he was expected to do. Worse, he would never admit to cowardice. Ever.

'All right,' she said. 'Here's the plan. We leave the gear here. The rope that I told you about is over there. See? That blue rope tangled up in the rocks. Way over?'

'Yes,' he said. 'Just.'

'One of us – me, if you like – goes across, gets that rope, knots one end to that tree stump there, then drags the other end back. We tie it around one of these rocks . . .' She indicated two or three boulders on the beach behind them. 'We make sure that it's good and tight, then we shoulder the gear and go over, using the rope to steady us. All right?'

'All right,' he said, making no attempt to do anything.

'You sure?'

'Yes.'

She took off her pack and he did the same.

'No,' she said. 'You can keep yours on. I only took mine off because I'm going over to get the rope.'

He watched as she walked off down the beach. He felt stupid. What was he here for? Just to carry the second pack when she came back with the safety rope? Was that all? Something stirred inside him, a feeling that he should be doing something and, before he knew it, he called, 'Mala . . .'

Perhaps there was an urgency in his voice; perhaps it was simply the first time he had used her name – but she turned around, expecting trouble. 'What?' she said.

'I want to go.'

'You will,' she assured him. 'Once I get the rope.'

'No,' he said, coming up to her. 'I mean now. First. Let me do it.'

'It's a man's job is it?' She threw her head back and laughed. 'Sure, go right ahead. But you need to be able to tie a knot. Can you do that? A good scout's knot?'

Now he laughed. 'Yeah,' he said. 'Right. You can just see me going to scouts. I'd really fit in, wouldn't I? 'Course I can tie a knot. You'll see . . .' And he jogged off down the beach, every bit the man – though he entered the water with a little more delicacy.

He crossed the submarine causeway without difficulty, even stopping once, about half-way, to look back at Mala. He waved and went on. When he reached the other side he tied the rope off, as promised, then set out on the return. This was not so easy. The rope was heavy and too long to be wound in manageable coils. It was necessary to drag it behind him and with the weight, and the fact that it was caught by the sea and washed about or tangled around rocks, he soon found himself in trouble. And not just with the rope. The waves broke around his legs, some reaching his waist, but he went on, and was just about to flash her a grin at having made it when he lost his footing and fell into the sea.

He broke the surface gasping. His feet were on the bottom, but the undertow through the passage was so strong that he feared he would be swept away. The rope was no longer in his hand and he lunged forward, panicking, to feel the skin on his palm tear as he grasped a rock. Then Mala was above him, her hands extended, and he clasped them both as she pulled him up into the sun.

'I'm sorry,' he said, shaking himself. 'Honest, I am. And I dropped the rope.'

'The rope's not going anywhere,' she said and although he failed to realise it, she did not release her grip until they stood on the sand.

'Wait,' she said simply. He watched as she took off her shorts and waded into the water to salvage the drifting rope, hauling it in, metre after dripping metre, until there was enough to tie it off on a rock. 'There.' She wiped the weed and water from her hands in a business-like way. 'That should do it. Now, where's my helper?'

He felt worse, having been no help at all, but he got up and slipped on his pack, following her lead.

'I guess you know why that rope's across now,' she said as they walked towards the water. 'Believe me, I wouldn't attempt to go over with my gear if it wasn't there.'

'But what if I fall in again?' he asked. 'Or drop a camera in?'

'You won't. Anyway, you're only carrying the accessories in that bag. Film. Extra lenses. Binoculars. And it's supposed to be waterproof. Or so the label says. But this one . . .' she patted the bag on her back, 'it's got both my cameras in it. If it goes under, that's a different matter.' As she spoke she stepped out onto the first rock, her hand gripping the rope beside her. He followed, conscious of his responsibility, and step by step they made their way across.

'All right,' she said when he finally joined her. 'All right,' and she reached out to pinch his cheek as if he were a baby. 'No noise, now, OK? Pretty soon we've got a parrot to sneak up on.'

Ordinarily he wouldn't have let himself get involved in a situation like this, but here he was, soaked to the skin, lugging somebody else's stuff and getting ready to photograph a bird. He shook his head in bewilderment – yet raised his hand to his cheek to touch the spot where she had pinched him.

The path that they followed led gradually upwards, twisting and turning through wind-blown coastal scrub, until it appeared to vanish into a cavernous natural arch.

Mala went straight on but the boy hesitated, looking about to see if there was some other way.

When she realised that he was not behind her, she came back to the entrance to find him. 'What's up?' she asked.

'Nothing,' he muttered. 'It's nothing . . .' Yet for the second time that day she saw his hand reach up to his hair, pulling it down over his eye.

'You sure?'

'Yep,' he assured her. 'Go on,' and he followed her into the gloom, still stroking his hair.

It was not dark for long. In a minute they were through and there was the path again, leading up towards the domed summit of the headland, a bare granite knoll about a hundred metres above the waves. When they reached it, and had stopped to rest, Mala pointed towards a gully thick with banksia and heath that lay between them and the sea. 'Believe it or not,' she said, keeping her voice low, 'the nest is in there. Once we leave here, no talking. Sign language only, OK?'

He nodded. Not talking didn't bother him a bit.

'There's a well-camouflaged depression a few metres from the nest itself. If we can slip into that quietly we should get a couple of good shots of the fledglings. Unzip that accessories bag now and leave it open, facing me, so I can dig into it if I need to. And remember: keep quiet.'

He followed her again, trying all the while not to laugh. This was crazy. The silliest thing that he had ever done, yet he was still following.

When they reached the gully she dropped to her knees, took a camera from her pack and crawled into the undergrowth, where she lay still. Simon watched carefully then did likewise, stretching out beside her. When he had settled she reached into his bag and removed a pair of field glasses which she placed at the ready, but he could make out nothing worth looking at – only the sandy bed of the gully, a few stunted bushes and the odd pile of dead grass and leaves – until she nudged him and inclined her head towards the nearest of the bushes. 'Down there,' she breathed.

Then he saw. Three baby birds lay in a dip in the sand. Ugly things they were, their feathers so dark they could be mistaken for shadow – which was why he had not seen them – their biscuit-coloured beaks wide open and gasping at the air. There was no real nest, nothing like one, but when he nudged her to let her know that he had seen them she was already busy focusing her camera, so he let her be. For a while she clicked away, then she turned to him again and whispered, 'I might get the hen. Don't move.'

So they waited. For ten minutes. Twenty minutes. A half hour. He could not remember having been so still for so long. He watched a green-and-red beetle crawl over his hand in what seemed to be a life journey. He felt something – an ant, he hoped – creep across the back of his neck. Sweat dropped from his nose and vanished into the sand. But he did not move. Not once. Out of respect for her he did not move a muscle.

Then the hen came. Or a bird that he took to be the hen. It was a pretty thing, not a bit like he had imagined from her description, and for the first time it made sense that someone was trying to save it. It was so small. So frail. It could never save itself. Slowly, so as not to be noticed, he turned to Mala. He could see the veins pulsing in the back of her hand as she steadied the camera. He sensed the pressure she sustained on the shutter until the precise moment when the bird bent over the chick to feed it and he felt the release as she pressed the shutter home. And then the bird was gone. In a flurry of wings it was suddenly gone.

He touched Mala's arm to ask what was happening, but she was too taken up with the camera and attempted to satisfy his curiosity by shoving the field glasses in his direction with her elbow. He did not pick them up. She tried again, all the while keeping her hands firmly on the camera. But when he ignored her a second time, she put the camera down and glared at him, as if to say 'What's the matter with you?'

He raised his hand and lifted the hair that covered his fixed and sightless eye.

She bit her lip. 'Here,' she whispered and, reaching into

the bag that he had carried, she withdrew a cylindrical case of black leather. 'Open it.'

Inside was a camera lens.

'It's telephoto,' she whispered. 'It might help.' And, as Simon put it to his eye, the mother bird returned.

It was noon by the time Mala had finished her shoot on the headland and after two when she and Simon returned to the shack. 'I've got a bit of a makeshift dark-room down in the back shed,' she said. 'How about coming down with me to see how these shots turned out?'

The boy turned pale. 'I'll be OK here,' he answered. 'Honest.'

'But . . .'

'No,' he said. 'I'm fine.' His hand went straight to the lock of hair that fell across his eye. He caught it in his fingers and twisted it like a nervous child.

There could be no doubt that he felt threatened but, for the life of her, Mala could not work out why. 'Sure,' she said, 'sure . . .' and turned to leave him. At the back door she looked back, calling, 'You can fix yourself something if you're hungry. There's plenty of bread and some cold meat in the fridge.'

Simon was happy to be alone. When she had gone he

went into the kitchen and made himself a sandwich and a coffee, which he took onto the verandah. He sat in the same cane chair that she had occupied and ate with his feet up on the rail. When he had finished he peered out to sea through the lens she had lent him, and then he got up, leaving it on the railing, and wandered down to the beach.

He looked to the right and to the left. Either way there was only sand. He had been to the left with her that morning and, though he suspected that he would see much the same whichever way he went, he turned to the right.

He walked barefoot, kicking the soft sand ahead of him and sometimes, where it had baked into biscuity layers, it cracked beneath him and lifted. Once he looked back and imagined that he was a giant walking over the face of the earth and that these fragments he was forming with his massive steps were new continents. He wondered what he would name them, since he had created them, but decided that such places were better left un-named and so forever free, as he hoped that he would be.

He thought also of this Mala Glass woman and the time he had spent with her, and of the man Greg Muir, who had taken him on, and where he was coming from and what he was trying to prove, and he laughed a little to himself – even though he was sure that 'his heart was in the right place', as people so often said about men like him – but when he thought about Mala he could not laugh.

She had a way of getting him to do things that he would never have done for anybody else. He couldn't say that it was just a sex thing, because he had known about sex one way and another since he was fourteen, so it had to be more than that. When it came down to it, he had to admit, there was something about her that he liked. And about Muir too. Something about them both that he couldn't shake off. It was as if he had no choice.

He was wrestling with these things when he heard what he thought was the tinkling of tiny bells. He stopped and looked. Above the dunes that separated the beach from the interior he saw a flock of multicoloured parrots wheel and rise, circling higher and higher until they crossed the disc of the sun and were gone.

He wondered what it was that had set them calling and flying in such a way and left the beach to climb the rippled dunes, leaning forward to compensate for the incline, the shift and slide of the sand, finally dropping to his knees to peer over the top.

He could see nothing that might have startled the birds; nothing that might have even attracted them in the first place, no tree or pool or patch of seeded grass, and he wondered if he had seen and heard them at all – if he wasn't touched by the sun – but as he was about to leave he noticed something strange at the base of the next dune: a circle, he thought, like a position marker for the dropping of supplies from an aircraft, or a target for a military exercise.

He regretted having left the lens on the verandah at the shack and moved to a better spot.

Below him was a circle of sticks about three metres in diameter and, within that, another circle, like a satiny blue-black cloth thrown down upon the sand. In its centre were what seemed to be four white stones, each the size of a football, giving the whole the appearance of a massive nest. He had to get closer, and since there was no sign of anyone about, he slithered down the dune on his backside.

The sticks around the outside of the circle touched end to end except for a gap about a metre wide directly opposite him; but whether this was deliberately left, or whether the maker of the circle had simply run out of sticks, the boy had no way of knowing. The central disc, which had seemed blue-black and shining, was only charcoal, no piece bigger than his fist, but it was the white, egg-shaped stones that really took his eye. If they were in fact stones, which he still could not tell. He got up and stepped into the circle, intent on picking one up. As he did, the sound of tinkling bells came again and just as suddenly the parrots swooped low over his head. He ducked instinctively and when he looked up he saw a man with three camels in train watching him from the edge of the circle, at the gap where it had not been closed.

For a moment he thought this was a vision – as when he had first seen the parrots wheel – but it was no vision. The man released the camels, dropping the plaited thong that held them, and moved silently around the sticks so that Simon was forced to turn also, to keep his eye on him, but the man himself did not look up.

He was very old. His skin was dark and weathered, his silver-white hair caught up beneath a head-scarf of deepest blue. He wore a waistcoat of ragged tapestry, a patched and faded shirt, and his trousers – likewise patched and faded – hung from a cord of leather knotted around his narrow waist.

'Who are you?' Simon asked. 'What do you want?' Then the man stopped and turned to him and Simon saw that his eyes were honey coloured and soft.

'Tell me,' the boy pleaded. 'Tell me what you want . . .' In answer the man looked up, catching Simon's eye, penetrating his armour of self as no-one had ever done, and the boy was filled with fear.

Without a word Simon turned and ran. He ran through the dunes until he reached a gap that led to the beach and here he stopped and looked back once to see that he was alone. Then he walked on to the shack as casually as he could.

Mala found Simon sitting on the verandah. She asked him if he was all right and when he assured her that he was she showed him the photographs that she had taken that morning, laying them out on a table, detailing their strengths and weaknesses, one by one.

Again Simon was struck by how she managed to draw him in, and why he bothered to listen, but he did, and the afternoon passed without his knowing until something – the sound of distant bells, he thought – made him lift his head. There on the beach were three camels, walking one behind the other, with the old man leading them.

'That's Atman,' Mala said. 'He collects native flowers. See? They're strung on the backs of the camels, hanging down to dry. All sorts he gets. Certain species nobody has ever seen before. Heaven knows where he goes to get them. Way up north, they say, some secret place. He trades them for goods at a dealer in Esperance. Here . . .' She reached out to the verandah rail to pick up the tele-photo lens. 'Have a look. You'll see him much better.'

But Simon shook his head and turned his attention back to the photographs.

Shane Rowe
Senior Editor
Rare Earth
PO Box 74
Perth WA

8 October

Dear Shane

How are you? I'll enclose the last of the ground parrot photographs, which I've just finished developing. They're mostly of the new chicks. From what I can see (they're still drying) I'm pleased with them! Also, here's the draft of my accompanying article. Any changes will have to wait till I get back from the trip – I hope that's OK with you?

Speaking about the trip, we're almost ready to go. Greg and the boy arrived yesterday, and Greg's in town right at this moment, getting some last-minute supplies. If all goes to plan, we should be leaving sometime tomorrow morning.

Greg does look older – a bit thicker around the waist and there's a touch of grey creeping in at the temples – but I have to admit, Shane, it was good to see him again. When they first arrived he seemed distant, not very excited to see me at all. In the evening, though, he volunteered to cook dinner, a little celebration of our reunion, I guess, which was a nice gesture. I hope we've both matured since we were last together and things between us won't be so disastrous.

I've just spent the morning with Simon, the kid who's come along with Greg. He seems pretty smart, if a little green, but then what else should I expect from a sixteen-year-old? He's good-looking, a bit scruffy, as boys of his age are, and big. He's nearly as big as Greg. Greg's taken him on as part of some welfare scheme, but it's hard to imagine why. Apparently he's a runner, takes off from everywhere. Greg says his parents are OK and no one, not even the social workers, can work out why he keeps running. I think he's got a chip on his shoulder because of his eye – he's got a glass eye – but I guess there must be more to it than that.

I'd better finish now and I'll try to get this parcel off to you first thing tomorrow – hope you like the pics!

Love,

Mala

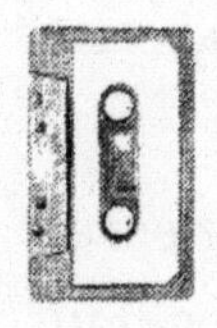

9 October

Hello, Shane

All of a sudden I've got some spare time, so I thought I'd start a tape to you. Greg's taken himself off somewhere and Simon is still curled up in his sleeping bag, out to the world.

Greg and I had a good talk last night about this trip. We don't see any problems at Cape Le Grand, but if we head north an extra person might put a strain on our stores, especially the water. Greg said he's already had a few words with Simon about the need to conserve it. There's supposed to be a well just south of the El Dorado sapphire mine, which is close to where we want to explore, but since the maps are based on data that's thirty years old, it's too risky to rely on them totally.

About the Wazo, this is basically what we've got to go on so far, as I've outlined to Greg. People claim to have seen it around Esperance more or less since the arrival of the first Europeans, and the sightings have arisen about every twenty years, though it's only ten years between the last two reports. The reports come from two main areas – one is the coast of the Recherche

Archipelago and the other is to the north, a much vaguer area.

The hang-gliders at Hellfire Bay, Gwen's experience at Mississippi Point and the further report off Mondrain Island are the strongest leads we have. They indicate that we are looking for a coastal bird. The sealers' stories support this idea as well.

But other tales suggest a land or desert bird! Some descriptions mention the old sapphire mines, which are two hundred to three hundred kilometres north nor'-east of here. A tourist couple reported seeing it east of Salmon Gums where, they said, it was gliding over a range reputed to be extremely barren. Then there was the botanist, Abrahams, who found remnants of an enormous egg-shell, twenty-three centimetres in diameter and thirty-eight centimetres long. He was in the same area, a little east of the range, verging on the desert.

Greg and I have talked about the logical possibilities. My hunch is that it's a case of amateurs not recognising birds we know exist. To start with, it could be the *Diomedea exulans*, the wandering albatross. We know that they venture north into the Recherche Archipelago between July and November. They're the largest albatross, with a wing-span of up to three-and-a-quarter metres, and they're well over a metre long, which is much bigger than any of our raptors.

Or it could be *Fregata andrewsi*, the Christmas Island frigate-bird. It's another large bird, though not as big as the albatross, which could have been blown off course in a storm. But Greg thought it was highly unlikely that it would be so far out of its range.

The southern giant petrel, *Macronectes giganteus*, is another possibility. Some of these people could have been scared by the look of it scavenging out at sea. The nostril tubes along its beak and its hunched back can make it look really sinister. People could have been frightened and started to fantasise. Why not?

Of course, our biggest inland bird is the wedge-tail eagle, but it's so easily identified, I doubt if that's what people have seen. Anyway, the only reason I can think of why any of these birds would attack a human would be to defend a nest. But even that's very unusual.

Gwen said the bird that attacked her carried away an adult seal, not a pup, and had a wing-span of about twenty metres. I know things can seem enormous when you're a child, but even a scared kid can see that the length of a bed is different from the length of a tennis court. So, if we say, for argument's sake, that Gwen's twenty metres is an exaggeration, even if we halve it, ten metres is still significantly bigger than any bird living today.

The colour is what convinces me that we are not talking about a single bird species. So far it has been reported to be the colour of water, and invisible in the sky. Does that make it greenie-blue or grey or white?

Even though I can't explain the differing versions of the bird's colours, or the sightings so far inland, I still say we're looking at an albatross or a petrel defending its young. Greg is not so sure. He reckons many of these people are locals, used to seeing albatross, petrels and sea eagles, and he reminded me that the woman with the sad eyes said, 'my father knows his birds, and this ain't one he knows'. So it's certainly a mystery to be solved, which makes me all the more keyed up and ready to go!

Talk again soon.

That final night at the cottage Simon slept badly, his mind filled with images of Atman and the circle of sticks in the dunes. He woke the next morning feeling irritable and unsettled, and he knew that if he was going to make some sense of what had happened, or at least clear the episode from his head, he would have to return to the place for another look.

He went into the kitchen and made his coffee then looked around for the others. This was the day they were due to leave. Mala was busy packing her gear while Muir was on the verandah looking through maps and making notes in his journal. Satisfied that he could slip away without any trouble, the boy crossed the yard and turned towards the dunes. He hadn't gone twenty metres before Muir called him. He stopped and looked back.

'Where are you going?' Muir asked.

'Just along the beach.'

'Yes, but where? In case we need you.'

'Where I went with Mala yesterday.'

This was a lie and as soon as he said it he knew that he had made a mistake.

'What? Mississippi Point? You're headed in the wrong direction. It's that way. To the east.'

The boy struck his forehead, feigning stupidity, and was about to turn when Muir crossed to the verandah rail. 'Simon,' he said, 'can you use a compass?'

'Not sure.'

'Is that a yes or a no?'

'No.'

'Well, I'd say it's time that you learnt. We're going into some pretty tough country on this trek and I don't want you getting lost. Like it or not, I'm responsible for you, remember. Come on up here.'

When Simon had joined him at the table Muir produced a compass and held it out to him. 'This is an orienteering compass. See the cord? That's to wear it around your neck. It's easy to use, if you watch and listen, and it could save your life. Here's what you do . . .'

He unfolded a map and laid the compass on it. 'First we put the compass on the map with its straight edge pointing north. Then we turn the map to align north on the map with the north point on the compass. We hold the compass capsule steady and rotate the direction arrow to the path we're going to take. We read off the degrees of difference between true north and where we're going. That way, if we lose a visual landmark we can simply put our compass on the map and plot our direction by reading the degrees on the compass dial. Easy.'

Simon nodded, though he had understood nothing. There was something about the compass itself that intrigued him – its shape; its intricacy – but little else. He had never been one for direction. When his time came to go – to run – he simply went. Who cared if it was north, south, east or west? Even now, he saw a chance to go – go altogether, anywhere – and he said, 'Great! Thanks, Greg. Could I have a try now? Along the dunes? By myself?'

'Why not?' Muir shuffled through the maps and spread one on the table. 'This is where we are. The best idea is to choose something as your marker, something high – like the chimney on the shack – and keep that in sight. See how you go. You can have the compass. You never know . . .'

Simon thanked him and headed off through the dunes, but the moment he was out of sight he slipped the compass cord around his neck and forgot all about it. When he was certain that Muir couldn't see him, he dropped back down to the beach and headed in the direction he had taken the day before.

At first he scanned the sand above the tide-line, looking for the footprints of the camels, but he could see none. He looked towards the sand hills, watching for something familiar, something that reminded him of where he had climbed up when he had first heard the birds and seen them swoop and climb. Try as he might, he could see nothing. Each dune looked the same.

And then, when he would have turned back, since he had no clear idea of why he was doing this anyway, what exactly he was trying to prove, he felt a sudden tightening in his stomach, a sudden nervousness, as if he were being watched, and he knew that he had reached the place.

He glanced back once to assure himself that he was alone, then veered sharply off the beach and climbed the nearest dune. He looked over and there was the circle, just as he had seen it the day before. Once more it seemed to call him and once more he slithered down to stop at its edge of sticks.

He felt different now, assured that he was alone. He got up without hesitation and stepped into the circle. He bent and touched the four egg-shaped stones and satisfied himself that they *were* in fact stone. He even allowed himself a smile at the possibility that they could have been anything else, considering their size. As he stood up, convinced that he was surveying the work of a crazy man, the feeling that Atman was nearby came over him again and he looked back towards the centre of the circle. Within the tell-tale compass of the stones, he thought he saw movement. He dropped to his knees in the ash and leaned forward, turning his head to see, as was his way. There was something . . . A piece of driftwood had been pressed into the sand and, attached to it by a plait of silver hair, was a single, deep-blue feather.

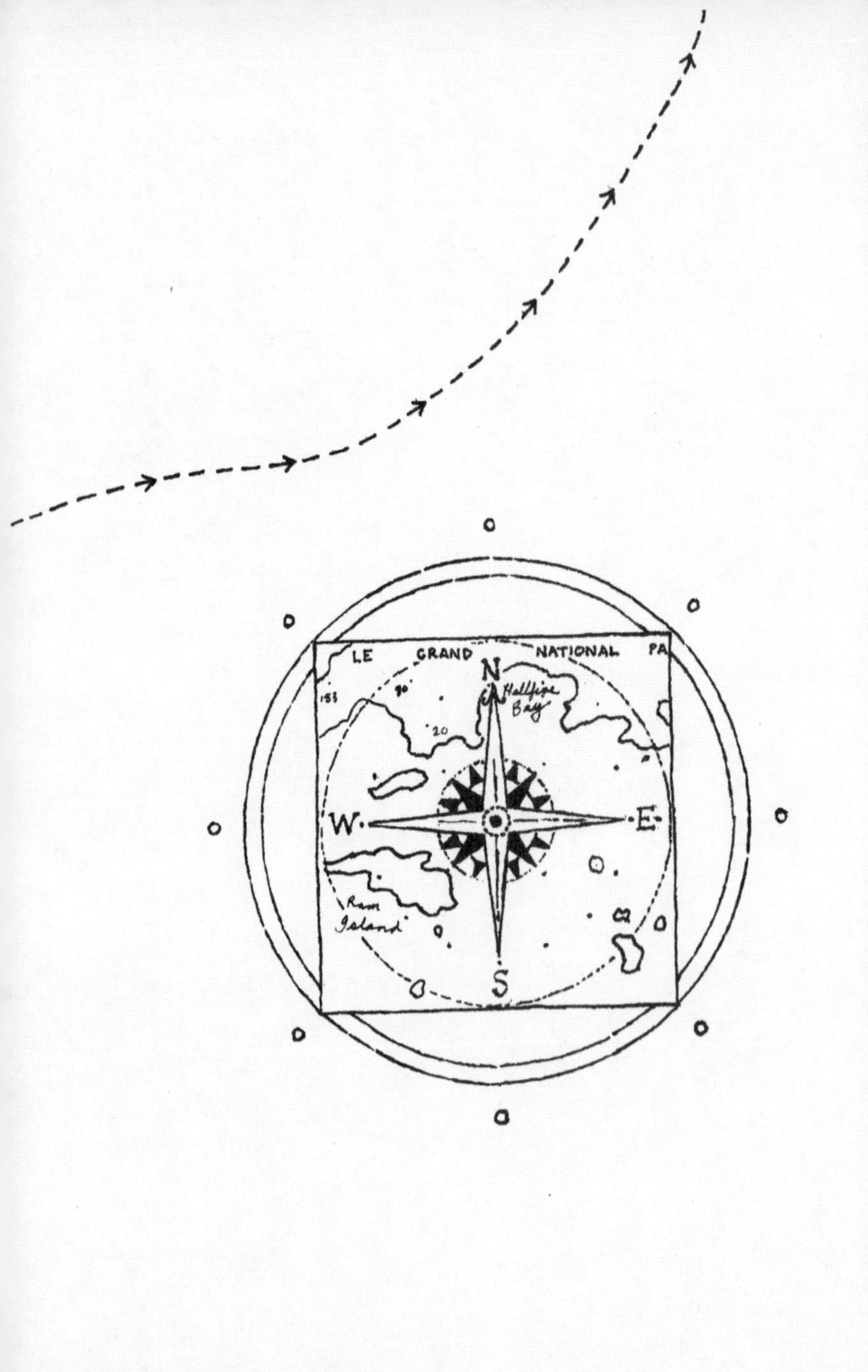
LE GRAND NATIONAL PA
N
Hellfire Bay
W
E
S
Ram Island

9 October

Hi, Shane – how's it going? We've finally arrived at Cape Le Grand. I always get a thrill at the start of a field trip, it's the real start of the project for me. Camp has just been set and I've come down to the beach to be alone and report in.

It's beautiful here, Shane. I was thinking, if I don't get enough action shots hunting for 'the bird', I could do a side-line of Australiana cards, it's that stunning. The coastline is still dominated by the same great granite boulders as at Esperance, but here the harshness of the dry, open scrub between those grey outcrops is countered with delicate flowers of butter yellow, royal purple and rusty red. We're camped fifty metres from the beach, just the other side of a tea-tree thicket. And what a beach! The sand is startling white, the sea, even at this late hour of the afternoon, is bright turquoise.

Though Cape Le Grand is only two hundred kilometres from Esperance, it took us the whole day to get here. We didn't start packing till fairly late and having a third person significantly increased the load. It's not just an extra body with a pack, it's also fifty percent more food and as much water as we can possibly carry. Fortunately we're able to store some gear in the dinghy. By the time we headed out, Greg's station-wagon looked like those donkeys you see labouring under impossibly large loads. The drive was slow anyway because the track isn't used much, except by those ill-fated hang-gliders and the police, so it's very rough and in parts non-existent. At one stage we headed off in the wrong direction and wasted over two hours before we eventually got back on the right track. Then we came to a stretch of soft sand and tried to go around it through the scrub, but as we did one of the tyres blew out – pierced by a dead branch. I'll tell you, the mood in the car was not helped when Greg went to fetch the kangaroo jack off the roof-rack and found it wasn't there. Apparently, in the morning when Simon was helping us pack, he thought he would get it out of the way and so he stowed it underneath everything in the back. We ended up having to unpack then repack almost everything just to change the tyre.

The only redeeming feature of the drive was that I talked to Simon. He was asking questions about me and my work. He wanted to hear all about the assignments I've done and the 'exotic' places I've been to, and he kept talking about my 'sense of freedom' – interesting.

Greg hardly said much to him the whole day. I'd have thought he'd make more of an effort, you know, joke around with him or something. I was watching them just now as they were rigging up the tarpaulins for our shelter. Simon was helping stretch the tarp and tie the leads to the stakes. When Greg was done on his side he came across to check how securely Simon's knots were fastened and found them wanting. I don't know what Greg said, but I could see Simon recoil, either from failure or embarrassment, and then turn defiantly angry when Greg tried to show him what to do. I hope for the kid's sake Greg knows what he's doing, because at the moment they're miles apart.

Well, Shane, thanks for listening. I'm off for a walk now, after all that driving.

10 October

Shane, hello again. I've been looking at the 'incident statement' I was given by the police back in Esperance. It says the two hang-gliders had been camped at Hellfire Bay and were spending their days scuba diving and hang-gliding which they did from the headland at the eastern end of the bay, landing on the beach. At the time of the 'accident', the survivor said his friend was following the coast east towards Lucky Bay while he was flying out over the water. He was on the return, cruising north towards land for a minute or two, enjoying the twilight sky, and he could see the lime green and orange wings of the other glider in front of him. Just as he was banking around to go back out to sea one last time, he swears he saw a huge bird, as big as the glider, arrowing down as if it was attacking. His friend had no chance to see the bird as it was coming at him from behind. That sounds reasonable to me – raptors do attack from the prey's blind spot. That's no big deal. But I'm not convinced about the bird's size.

Anyway, the guy yelled to his friend to warn him but it was no use, they were too far apart, and by the time he'd turned his glider around, the other one had already crashed. The bird took off with the victim in its talons. As it did, the glider tumbled over the precipice into the sea.

The pilot was afraid for his own safety by now, and there was nowhere close by for him to land, so he headed back to Hellfire Bay and drove to Esperance to get help.

This morning we went to check out the crash site, which was only four kilometres from our camp. We decided to follow the coast, imagining it would be easier than trying to bush-bash through the waist-high scrub. We found that we had to rock-hop for over three hours, up and down the steep granite spurs that lie side by side like giant fingers in a never-ending line. At the same time we had the sun full on our backs and the black rock radiating the heat into our faces.

By the time we reached the site of the crash, the giant spurs had finally given way to sheer cliffs. We dropped our gear and clambered around the top of the cliffs where Greg found two marks. They were half-way down the eastern face of one of the peaks. One was a short, deep gouge and the other looked as if a chunk had been struck off the cliff face. The indentations were still white, suggesting they had been made recently, and their size indicated a fair amount of force. After hitting the cliff, the hang-glider must have then slid down the ten-metre drop into a small valley. We could see drag marks and scratches at the bottom where the granite gave way to sand and limestone rubble. Further into the scrub there were a number of broken branches and squashed bushes where something heavy had been lying.

The sergeant believes, and I tend to agree with him, that the wind must have caught the sails and blown it over the edge. Greg disagrees. He said that if the wind was coming off the sea, which was most likely, it would have blown the craft further inland, not back towards the sea and over the cliff. After seeing the layout of the terrain, I think the glider could have been blown either way.

Simon tried to join in when we were picking through the stones and plants, and kept asking us what we could read from them. He seemed amazed that evidence of what had happened there over a month ago could still be seen.

We also searched across the top of the cliffs. I abseiled down to a couple of ledges to see if anything had lodged there and took some shots looking up at the site. Since I couldn't get any aerial views, I hope these will convey some of the drama.

If only we'd known the hike was going to take so long we would've been prepared to sleep out on the cliffs. Since we'd miss the dawn, we decided to wait for dusk to watch the sky before heading back to camp. I was surprised at Simon, though, he became very tense and started to argue with us. He wasn't interested in the sunset or the birds, he just wanted to get going. When Greg and I refused he went off and sat in a sulk. On the way back he always seemed to be in my way and I kept treading on him. It was so different from the morning when we just saw the back of him as he led the way.

Our only excitement, watching the sky, came from a pair of osprey cruising the coast. Greg and I agreed they were very unlikely to be the culprits. In all, we didn't find any other evidence of the hang-glider or pilot, nor of anything unusual.

Well, Shane, I'm ready to crawl into my sleeping bag. Good night.

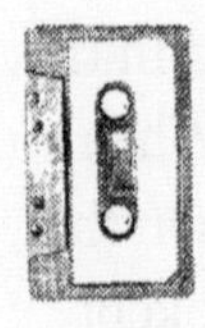

11 October

Shane, I'm so glad I have you to talk to – or complain to in this case! I can't moan to Simon, and I've already had a go at Greg. I was furious with him this morning. He got out the maps and announced that we should make our way over to the coastal hills today. I said, 'What about the hang-glider? We haven't even spent a full day looking for it,' but he said that there was no point since the police had already combed the area for three days and found nothing. I wasn't going to let him get away with it. I told him straight out not to forget that I was in charge of this project, and that I wasn't ready to abandon the coastal search yet – that I intended to be thorough and I needed to look for wayward debris from the hang-glider or an albatross's nest, at the very least.

Greg got me there, though. He reminded me that albatrosses make their nests from mud and tussock grass. Obviously they fly these waters in the colder months and a colony wouldn't choose a place like this to nest.

Greg now seems convinced that the Wazo isn't a *Diomedea*, a *Macronectes*, nor any other kind of seabird. He thinks it's a raptor. Therefore we should be looking for a cache – a place where raptors hide their food when it's too big to carry to the nest. These caches, like their nests, are always found in high places, which make the hills that dot this area the obvious locale to search – according to Greg. What do you think of that? He actually believes this bird exists!

Anyway, I won the argument and we've been making our way at an easy pace along the coast in the dinghy. At the moment we've stopped for lunch in a protected little cove, which is also home to a pair of Cape Barren geese. The swell is starting to build so I think we're going to have to turn and head back to camp empty-handed, no special shots and no further information.

I know one person who thinks I made the right decision. Simon is pleased we didn't hike today. Clambering up and down the steep rocks put a lot of pressure on his ankles and so they're really sore. He's a funny kid. He made me swear that I wouldn't tell Greg.

Well, I'd better stir the others so we can head off. Love from me – sorry for giving you an ear-full!

14 October

Hi, Shane. I haven't had time to talk to you over the past two days – we've been trawling the shoreline, which proved to be fruitless. Today I agreed with Greg that we could begin looking among the hills inland for signs of a cache or a nest. We managed to walk over two of the peaks, both about 350 metres high. In the process we came across a family of wallabies, a dugite and two tiger snakes, which immediately made me think of you: knowing how much you hate snakes, I bet you're pleased you're two thousand kilometres away!

Relations between Greg and me have settled down again. I started thinking that I was too hard on him when we argued the other day but, let's face it, he's a grown man; he should be able to handle criticism. As for Simon – why are boys so hopeless? Every day now we've been out in the sun, and there are no trees except for the occasional grove of banksias, which give no shade, yet Simon has to be continually reminded to cover himself.

I wonder why he's come on this trip at all. It can't be that he wants to spend time with Greg – they're hardly close – and neither can it be out of appreciation of the environment. He never gets excited by anything we see in the bush and I can't imagine that it will be any different when it comes to looking for some non-existent bird. When he gets that vacant stare and plays with his fringe, which he does a lot, I can't help but think that he's getting restless.

15 October

Shane, I've finally got something exciting to tell you! We've even opened a couple of beers to celebrate. Today I decided that Greg and I should separate and search in different places as a more efficient way of covering the area. My first thought was for Simon to join me, since he seems more comfortable with me, but then I changed my mind and spent the day by myself. Greg brought Simon along, so Greg should take care of him.

I found what could be our first clue when I was on Frenchman's Peak. The almost perfect cone shape of this mountain meant I could see easily. There were no ledges, therefore no large nest. The summit was strewn with a dozen or so boulders that were like giant grey building blocks, so I sat down in the shade of one and took out my camera to check what sort of panorama I could get of the area. But what I found more interesting was the subtle patterns of the granite, the varied textures and light on the rock, creating tones of grey ranging from a deep blue to almost white. At one point I focused on the base of a rock and, despite its being in deep shadow, the surface was shining. I assumed it was wet slime, but then I saw something moving in the breeze.

I got up and went to have a closer look. It was some sort of dark blue material that had snagged at the bottom of the boulder. The piece was about a metre long and in shreds, as if it had been pulled and torn in all directions. It was that very light synthetic fabric, you know the sort I mean – it's shiny and super strong. The material is obviously not from the wings of the glider; it's too fine for that and the wrong colour. I would say from its texture that it came from a track-suit. The boulder was one of three that stood together in a semi-circle, leaning forward to create a kind of cave – the sort of place that a raptor would use as a cache.

In the end, none of us could find any other clues, no scrapings, no tell-tale faecal matter, no feathers. So, the plot thickens . . .

I'll bring you the next instalment as soon as it happens! Bye for now.

When the search for further evidence of the bird along the coastal cliffs proved useless, Mala suggested that they should continue off-shore. One of the sites chosen was Mondrain Island, a wind-driven granite outcrop of the Recherche Archipelago. 'I've heard that Mondrain is a fascinating place,' she told Simon as they loaded the dinghy. 'It was a whaling station from about 1910 until the mid '50s and the ruins are still standing. Then there's the nest.'

Ruins he could do without, but Simon had heard nothing about a nest. 'What nest?' he muttered, trying not to show too much interest.

Mala shook her head. 'Honestly, Simon,' she said, 'unless you start paying attention you're going to find yourself in trouble one day.'

He let this pass. He had been in trouble for as long as he could remember.

'The rumour is – and I'm really into testing rumour at the moment – that the big bird was seen there when the whaling station was in operation. I've talked to a couple of old salts who swear black and blue that this bird used to appear out of nowhere from time to time – intervals of up to three or four years – to feed on the cast-off blubber and offal. Greg thinks it might have, and I admit that if there were such a bird, its coming in for that sort of rancid waste makes sense, but there's been no word of a sighting since the station closed and that's over forty years ago. Still, fishermen reckon there's a huge nest over there. On the cliffs of the southern side.'

'Do you really believe that?' the boy asked. 'I mean, if there was, that it could be this bird's?'

'No,' she said, 'I don't even believe that there is a bird. But . . .' and here she tossed an armload of sleeping bags at him to stow in a locker, 'if there is, I score. And if there isn't, I still end up with one hell of a story.'

The dinghy was a basic aluminium runabout powered by an ancient outboard. With a southerly blowing, it belted and thumped every whitecap until the boy felt that his brain had broken loose in his skull. Muir was at the back steering. He spent most of his time staring at the sky, on the lookout for birds. Mala sat in the middle. She held her chin high and kept her face into the wind. Simon had no way of knowing if she did this because she was enjoying herself or simply to keep from throwing up.

The island was a monstrous hemisphere of grey granite rising baldly from the sea. The waves striking it reminded him of a game that he had seen played in a hostel once. The boys would run towards a wall and then leap at it from a certain distance to see whose hand could leave the highest mark. The waves were like that. All their efforts just as pointless.

As they drew closer, Muir asked them to watch out for a landing place and Mala spotted the bright yellow of a pocket-handkerchief beach between boulders that spilled into the sea. She yelled above the wind and pointed furiously until Muir finally noticed and swung the boat in that direction. The boy couldn't help but admire how skilfully and certainly this man manoeuvred to bring it in. He could never have done this himself – not between those rocks – not with his single eye.

But Simon didn't feel so warmly towards Muir when he was asked to jump into the icy water and haul the boat onto the beach. The jeans that he was wearing were all that he had brought, since he had been told to travel light, and while the others stepped out high and dry he was soaked. Right away he could feel the abrasion of sand and the sting of salt in his crotch.

Mala caught him adjusting his underwear and laughed. Muir heard her and laughed too, adding, 'Don't worry. Save you having to take a bath.'

Simon instantly regretted that he had come – would have left them then and there, would have cut and run – but here, on this island, he was trapped. So he gave them a silly grin and said, 'Yeah, right,' and reached into the boat to collect some gear. He could wait. He had learned to play that game years ago.

He followed them up the beach and through the windswept scrub until they reached a clearing littered with shards of brittle stone. At its farthest edge stood the ruins of a settlement, its buildings of splintered timber as drab and grey as the stone they rose from. All of a type they were, whether cottage or shed – all windowless and roofless and empty, yet still as sharply gabled and prissily upright as if momentarily expecting some in-coming rush of people from the sea who might fill them up and give them life and set them smiling. 'Like those houses you see in picture books,' he muttered, stopping to wipe salt from his eye, 'with faces like people . . .' The others exchanged glances behind him.

They established camp in the lee of the ruins to gain some protection from the wind, then set out to walk to the southern cliffs. Mala and Muir were happy. She had taken some good shots of the settlement and had high hopes of more, while Muir seemed to find everything about him a source of fascination and was constantly stopping to examine a nut-brown seed or tuft of withered moss or piece of sea-fractured shell, which he would sometimes note in his journal, or pocket with a smile.

But Simon dawdled behind, careless, until in negotiating a boulder he stumbled and sent a shower of rocks tumbling down towards the sea. He turned to watch them leap and bounce and, as he did, he glimpsed what appeared to be a crevasse piled high with mounds of silvered logs – ancient driftwood, he imagined. Without a thought for the others he broke through the scrub and dropped to his knees at the edge to see.

He guessed at once what lay below him. These were not the bleached and weathered trunks of trees, but the giant and long-discarded bones of whales, this chasm their land-locked grave, and he reached out to touch one, to feel its power – since it seemed impossible to him that anything so free in life could be utterly spiritless in death – but as he did he heard a sound and there was Muir, staring down, and Mala behind him, and here he was on his knees.

'I was just looking,' he muttered, hating himself for even offering the hint of an apology.

'Next time you go off by yourself,' Muir said, 'let us know. It's one of the basic rules – laws, if you like – of trekking. Of the bush. Right? And I think that leaning over a cliff as high as this is a lot more than "just looking". All it takes is for you to slip and . . .'

But Mala pushed past Muir and offered the boy her hand, helping him up. 'Leave him be,' she said.

So they walked on, this time positioning the boy between them, an arrangement that was made without his consent, although he had been aware for days that such things were established by nods or winks or similar gestures, which he was presumably too ignorant to understand, or blind to.

By mid-afternoon they had reached the southern side of the island. Here their path led along a causeway of tumbled boulders that formed a barrier between the boiling sea and the cliffs that rose in layered steps and ledges beside them.

'This looks good,' Muir said, stopping and pointing up. 'Thermal air currents rising off the hot surface of the island, good nesting sites among those ledges up there. Any self-respecting sea bird would love this place. Keep your eyes on those cliffs. If there is a nest it will be protected, tucked around one of those corners, not facing out into these southerlies. But you won't miss it. If it's our bird's, it will be enormous. A real sight to see.'

Mala smiled as if to say 'Dream on', but she kept her camera at the ready all the same.

Simon did not share in the excitement. The more he thought about it, the harder it was to understand why he was there. Why he had agreed to come at all. Or come so far. And yet, no matter how he tried to shake himself free – as he had done a hundred times before, and from company and circumstances far worse than this – he simply couldn't walk away. Right then, had he really wanted, he could have dropped his pack and taken off and neither of them could have caught him. Never. As for this being an island, he could have reached the boat long before them. And the car was still there, back on the mainland. That would be nothing for him to hot-wire. Nothing at all.

Yet he stumbled on from rock to rock, grappling with his thoughts, until he almost bumped into Muir, his hand shading his eyes, staring up. Protruding from a cliff ledge high above was a mound of sticks the size of a haystack.

'That's a nest?' the boy asked, incredulous.

Muir nodded.

'But is it the one you're looking for?'

'I don't know. I need to get closer. Need to see what's using it. If anything is. It might have been abandoned for years. Big raptors move on if there's no steady food supply. And since the whaling station's been closed for years . . . But whatever built this is – or *was* – one hell of a bird.'

'Well, there's only one way to find out,' Mala said, hitching her pack. 'You ready for a climb, Simon?'

The boy hesitated, not sure that she was serious. He was not afraid of heights, although even he could see that this was no easy climb. The cliff face was steep, almost vertical, the surface granite loose and dangerous and sure to shift and crumble beneath his feet. Still, he picked up his pack as a statement of his willingness, and prepared to follow.

But Muir would have none of it. 'Wait!' he called. 'No-one's going anywhere. Not yet.'

Mala turned slowly and deliberately to face him, her eyes bright with anger. 'You weren't talking to me then, were you?' Her voice was steady, her tone ice-cold.

Simon stopped too. He looked from one to the other, the hint of a smile at the corners of his mouth.

'I was trying to say . . .' Muir stammered.

She slipped the pack from her back and approached him, choosing to stand on a boulder that set her slightly above. 'It wasn't what you were trying to say that worried me. It was what you said. And how you said it. Don't talk to me like that, Greg. And that goes for Simon, too.'

'Mala . . .'

'No, don't "Mala" me either. Sometimes you get a bit too big for your boots, Greg. Just remember that we're not a pair of birds that you're training. We're people. You get my message. Now, what was it that you were trying to say?'

Muir looked away, out over the sea, and Simon saw him place the palm of his hand flat on his stomach as if to calm himself. Then the man turned to her and said, 'I don't think it would be a good idea for us to go up to the nest. To get too near to it, I mean. After what happened to that hang-glider . . . If this bird exists, and if it attacks humans – for whatever reason – the worst thing we could do is to threaten its nesting site. If it's there now, or if it came back while we were up there, one of us could end up dead. Splattered all over these rocks, like that pilot. That's what I was going to say.'

'So?' Mala prompted.

Muir glanced at his watch. 'It's just after two. I think the best thing is to find a spot where we can observe the nest without being seen ourselves. Somewhere among that scrub up there. If the nest is in use, the bird should come back before dark. That gives us a good four hours. If you're prepared to wait.'

Simon felt his heart sink, but once again he followed, stumbling over boulders and through the debris washed up by the sea, until they reached the base of the cliff. Here they began to climb, heaving themselves from ledge to ledge, until settling at last among a tangle of scrub on a rocky outcrop in view of the nest.

There he sat, as instructed, and waited. He was frowned at if he spoke. He was too cramped to move. He was hungry. He was thirsty. Which was his own fault, as Mala quickly pointed out when he asked for a drink – after all, she had given him the canteen that rattled about, empty, in the bottom of his pack – so he understood how Muir felt when he had been reprimanded.

But the end did come. Just when Simon thought he could take no more, a huge bird appeared directly above him, silhouetted against the afternoon sky.

'Look,' he said. 'Up there.'

As they followed his gaze, the bird descended, circling slowly, to settle on the edge of the nest.

'Is it the one?' he whispered. 'Is it?'

He saw them exchange glances, and knew that it was not.

'But look at the size of it!'

'It's big, all right, but it's not our bird,' Muir said. 'That's a sea eagle. A white-breasted sea eagle. The bird we're after could be three, even four times bigger than that. Maybe eight metres from wing tip to wing tip. So big it could carry off a human being. That bird up there, big and beautiful as it is, well, I reckon it would be hard pushed to take a baby seal.'

'And?' The boy saw them shoulder their packs.

'I guess we struck out. Sorry.'

'What?' he persisted. 'After all that, we just get up and walk away?' He could hardly believe that he was saying this, that he cared enough to ask, and he saw them look at each other, surprised.

'We can stay if you like,' Muir said. 'Mala's got her camera and I'd be happy to sit here all night and watch. It's one hell of a beautiful bird, even if it isn't ours.'

The boy heard but shook his head. 'No,' he said. 'We should get back. It's coming on dark.'

But as he walked, the sight of that eagle stirred an image of the nest of sticks laid out in the dunes. And the golden eyes of Atman. And that single feather, as blue as heaven, secret, in his pack.

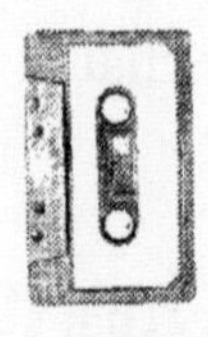

20 October

It's me again, this time from Mondrain Island. Yesterday morning we came over here in the runabout to have a look at a nest. Some fishermen had sighted a huge pile of sticks on the southern cliffs and told everyone it must be the Wazo's. What we found, of course, was the eyrie of a sea eagle.

The more I talk to people, the more I realise how easily they can be fooled. They want to believe in the rumour of the Wazo, so they talk themselves into seeing it. Even Greg. This morning he just went on and on about the thing.

You might say he was triggered off by what happened last night. We couldn't have been in bed long – I had already dozed off – when I was woken by strange noises. Paper was being ripped and things were being knocked over. I turned on my torch and caught sight of two monitor lizards having the time of their lives, tearing at bags and gorging themselves on our food. Someone, and I think it must have been Simon, had left the lid off one of the plastic containers we store our food in. Fortunately the culprits didn't have time to destroy too much.

Greg is really beginning to bug me. I had another go at him yesterday for the way he talks to us sometimes, so when he started going on about the monitors this morning, I wasn't in the mood. But I did well and held my tongue. He said that he had been thinking that if monitors feed at night, why couldn't our bird? He said that, Shane, our bird. He thinks it could be nocturnal, and it's true, owls are not the only raptors that hunt at night – letter-winged kites do, too. Greg thinks that would explain why the Wazo is seen so rarely, and that's how it protects itself. He brought up the case of the glider possum, which wasn't seen for over a hundred years and was thought to be extinct, but it survived because it only foraged after dark, when it was hidden and the forest was quiet. The same goes for the night parrot, come to think of it. And, Greg reckoned, with the size of 'our bird', if it did hunt by day it would have been shot out of the sky years ago. It would have been killed off, like the Moa, he said. Extinct. The Dodo. Extinct. He thinks that a very large animal like that needs to remain invisible to survive.

Then he went on to explain that if the bird is nocturnal and so big, its eyrie could be a hundred or two hundred kilometres away. The bigger raptors fly that distance in a matter of hours. If there is a Wazo, he reckoned, it could be hiding way up north in the desert where no human in their right mind ever goes, except loners like telegraph linesmen, prospectors and UFO crazies.

I am forcing myself to be a good scientist, Shane, and trying to keep my mind open to all possibilities. Even though Greg's facts are correct, it doesn't necessarily follow that a giant nocturnal raptor exists. But at this point I haven't got a better argument as to why we should stay down here near the coast, so I gave in and we're about to head north.

Bye for now.

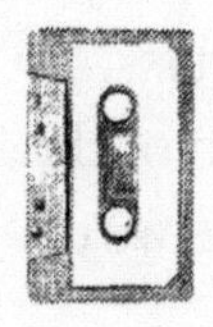

20 October

It's me again, Shane. I'm in my sleeping bag, wondering what am I doing here with two people who seem like strangers to me, and on a trip that I'm starting to suspect is going nowhere! I feel decidedly dirty and am struggling to resist scratching myself all over. At this particular moment I would be happy never to speak to anyone again – except you, of course.

The day started in an ordinary way. Once back on the mainland, we began heading north. For the first couple of hours the track climbed gently until it spilled over into a vast, shallow basin where the scrub became spare and the dirt was speckled with tall spinifex. Again the journey was slow, as we had to roll the station-wagon carefully over the rocks and holes to save the sump from being smashed.

Simon and Greg were dozing while I drove. It was mid-afternoon and hot, you know that feeling when you're sticking to the seat and sweat trickles across your scalp? Well, that's when I came to a fork in the track. I veered left onto what I thought looked like a smoother path, over baked mud. For a moment it was fine and I picked up speed. But then we skidded as the hard surface peeled off to expose a moist black mass. When I tried to brake, the weight and momentum of the trailer swung us around and we jack-knifed. Once we'd stopped, the wheels sank to the axles.

We managed to unhook the trailer and push it back onto firm ground easily enough, but the station-wagon was going to be hard work. The mud almost sucked my boot off every time I lifted my foot to take a step. Simon, without thinking, attempted to move faster than the muck would let him and fell face first. The poor kid looked very embarrassed when he managed to stand up, caked in that black ooze.

I would have thought, with the car as badly bogged as it was, we would have all pitched in to get it free, but we always seem to complicate matters. When Greg couldn't find his tools he had a go at Simon about the mess he had made in the back and said how he ought to be more responsible for his belongings. Simon snapped back, 'This isn't my mess. It's you two who wanted to come out here, not me. And anyway, I'm not allowed to be responsible for myself. You're responsible for me, you and your report.'

All Greg could say was that we all have to learn to be responsible for ourselves in time, but Simon had stopped listening. Greg then started setting up a winch and pulley system. He didn't explain what he was doing, nor ask for any help, until he ordered me to work the winch.

I was so angry that I told him to do it himself. He was stunned and I can see now that he had no idea what he'd done to upset me. 'I can't do it myself,' he said, and went over to the trailer and squatted in its shade.

After a very long and quiet fifteen minutes I gave in. It was interesting, Shane, because we did end up working together. The boys dug out the mud from behind the tyres while I worked the winch. But the bad feeling between us was just as thick as the mud we were stuck in!

By the time the car was standing on solid ground we were black from head to foot. I went and got one of the jerry cans of water and began washing myself and my boots. I offered to pass the can to Greg but when he said, 'No thanks, we need to save the water for later,' I lost control and yelled at him, 'What is it with you? Why don't you just loosen up? We can't all be as perfect as you. We've got enough water for now and there's a well coming up soon.'

'We don't know,' he said, 'what the well is like, whether the water is drinkable, or if the pump even works,' and he continued scraping off the mud.

Simon stood between us, not knowing who to believe.

Since we lost a couple of hours getting clear of the bog we only drove on for another hour before stopping for the night. I don't think a word was said during the drive and I stared out the window most of the way. In that quiet it occurred to me that these must be the salt flats the women at the museum mentioned. I also wondered how wide the band of salt was, and how impenetrable. If the women were right, these bogs must stretch for hundreds of kilometres, which would create both a physical and psychological barrier between the farming country of Esperance and the land we are heading for further north.

But the truth is, Shane, all day this one thought has been running through my mind: 'I don't want to be here.' I've been wondering why I teamed up with Greg again. And what I've got to do with Simon. Why do I feel trapped, when this trip was my idea in the first place? What am I really achieving by this search? I'm not going to find anything anyway.

Shane, I'll finish now and try to sleep. You know, when I used to laugh at the silly superstitions of my grandmother, she would say to me, 'Mala, what matters most is that you find your *own* truth. Never stop searching for that.' I suppose that's what keeps driving me: my desire for the truth.

Goodnight, Shane.

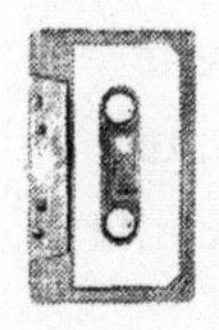

21 October

Hello, Shane. We're at the famous Well Number 234. Greg and I hardly said a word to each other all day and the drive here has been uneventful. Anyway, the well water is potable and all we need to do is turn on a tap. It's one of those old windmills that squeaks and groans as it pumps, as though it's exhausted with age and the harsh climate. There must be people out this way who still rely on its water, as I can see signs of makeshift repairs to the stand and tank.

Today Simon has been very annoying – behaving like a child. I was feeling tired and sweaty, and the dust had found its way into every nook and cranny. I asked Simon to help me fill the jerry cans with water. When I turned on the tap he made such a fuss, saying we couldn't drink it – it was too hot and rusty. I assured him it would be all right if we let it run first. He wasn't convinced and climbed up the tank to check inside for himself. One look at the slime around the edge and the rusted holes in the sides made him moan and carry on. I told him all water tanks out in the bush are like that, but he didn't know how to take me – whether I was teasing or not. The water pouring from the tap quickly cooled, though it was still tinged brown, and I went ahead and filled the storage cans and personal water bottles. Simon insisted on making silly faces when he filled his own.

After that I wanted to get cool myself, so I stripped off and climbed into the tank. It was great, so refreshing. When I got out Simon was just staring at me. I suggested that he should hop in. He went, 'Yuk. People are going to drink that water.' I didn't see any problem, I hadn't used soap. I told him that most people who pass through here would probably jump in and wash the dust off. He was so disgusted that he grabbed his water bottles and emptied them.

I couldn't let that go without giving him a lecture. I told him that there will come a time when he'd be so thirsty he'd have to drink whatever water was available, no matter what'd been in it, or where it came from!

Now we're on our way to visit a sapphire mine site and then we'll possibly go further north to the old telegraph station, but whatever we do it's going to be in this desert, and we'll be here for days. According to our map this is the last supply of water.

Love from me – I'll talk to you again soon.

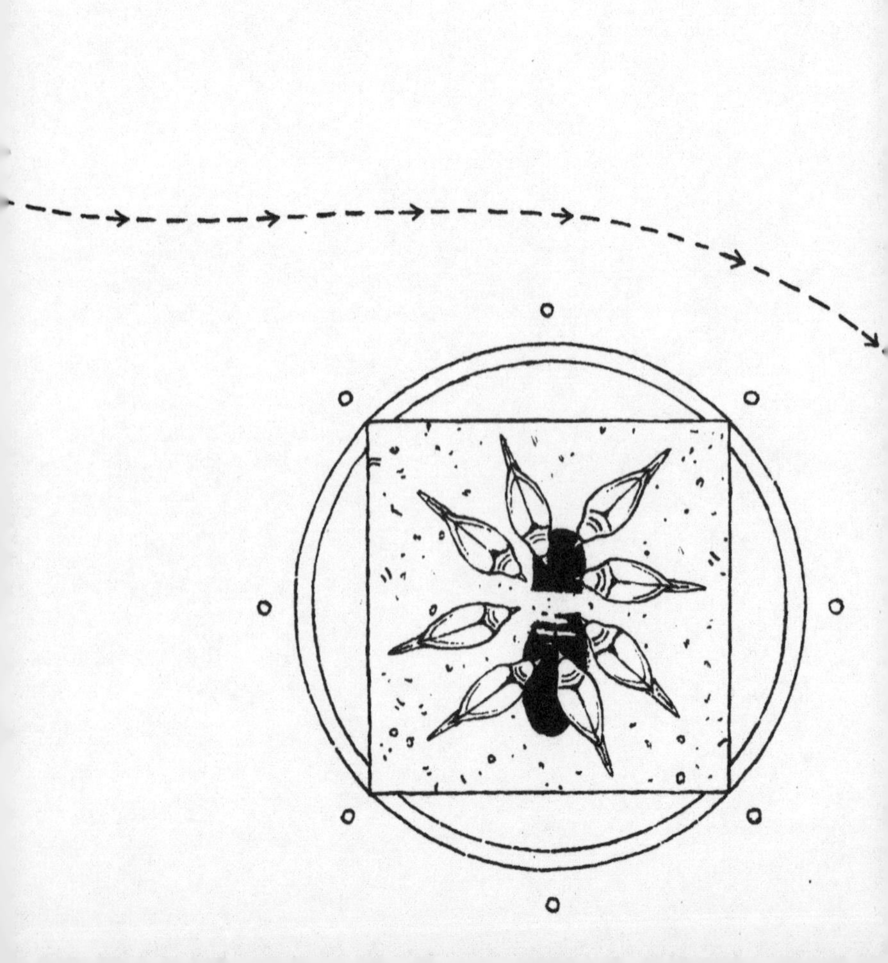

IT WAS COMING on night when they reached the El Dorado sapphire mine. Without being asked, Simon got out of the station-wagon and opened the gate to the property. It was clear from the state of the place that the mine wasn't exactly a roaring success, but there was smoke coming from the chimney of a galvanised iron lean-to at the back of a timber hut. Before Simon had a chance to step aside and let the car through, a grey-bearded man appeared at the door, a blue cattle dog beside him.

'What can I do for youse?' he called.

Simon pointed lamely towards the adults still in the car and the man stepped from the doorway and walked towards them, but the dog ran over to sniff the leg of the boy's jeans.

The dog was also one-eyed. Its right eye was black as coal, its left a lump of red-and-white flesh that reminded the boy of a marble he had once owned, formed from an agate. He was in a schoolyard, kneeling at the edge of a circle scratched in the dirt, and the agate was pressed between his thumb and his finger. Boys around the circle were shouting, 'Shoot, Dead-Eye. Go on, Dead-Eye. Shoot.' Hating the nickname as he did, the boy had thrown the agate down and left the game to hide and yearn for the sight that was lost to him forever.

The dog was nuzzling Simon's crotch as Mala got out of the car and introduced the three to the miner. 'We haven't come to jump your claim, or anything. We're on our way to the old telegraph station. We're gathering information on this big bird. This *oiseau* . . . or *Wazo*?'

She used these words with some hesitation, yet it was clear that the old man understood, since a gummy smile was immediately visible beneath his beard.

'The name's McTaggart,' he said. 'I been here thirty-two years. I don't get much company up this way, but youse are welcome to a cuppa tea.'

At this invitation they followed him into the hut. The walls were slabs of bark and sheets of rusted iron with yellowed newspaper and mud stuffed between. The floor was of tamped earth, also rust-red. There was only one room, at its centre a pine table and two pine chairs. In one corner stood a cast-iron bed of a type that the boy had slept in at a hospital once. There was not much else, save a cracked china basin with a blue-and-white enamel jug squatting on top of a lop-sided cabinet.

The visitors stood and waited while McTaggart disappeared behind a faded floral curtain that divided the interior of the hut from the lean-to where, from the sounds of tin and china clinking, they assumed that tea was being made. This proved to be true, since in no time he reappeared, ushering them all, sweating, back outside where he served them with chipped and stained cups of dark tea, without so much as asking if they wanted any, or how they wanted it, although even the boy was grateful for it. Mala smiled to herself, remembering the old women and their tea-drinking ceremony at the museum.

Next the miner brought out two chairs, one for Mala and, curiously, the other for himself. Muir and Simon had to be satisfied with sitting on the slab of stone that formed the doorstep.

McTaggart showed no interest in the nature of their visit, choosing rather to tell of his own purpose in being there and why he had chosen to stay so long. It was sapphires that he was after. Not the blue sapphire (which he treated with disdain) but a green-and-yellow form that he called parti-coloured, though not once did he produce any of these stones, which caused Simon to wonder if they existed at all. Like that big bird, he thought.

While McTaggart talked, the agate-eyed dog lay with its head on its paws, its sighted eye trained unflinchingly on Simon's, until the boy winked at the dog, who winked back as if to say, 'I know'.

It was Muir who finally suggested that they camp there the night. 'You don't mind?' he asked, and the old man laughed. 'So long as you don't try to share me bed,' was all he said.

McTaggart ate with them and afterwards returned to his hut to reappear with a tin of tobacco and a clay pipe, which he set about packing with such precise pressing and prodding that conversation ceased. When he was finished he broke wind loudly and with obvious satisfaction and then, turning to Mala, said, 'So you're after the bird, hey? The old Wazo?'

Muir's face was suddenly alive, but the question had not been directed at him. 'We are,' Mala answered, behaving as if this was exactly the cue she had been expecting. 'We heard that it was seen at the Overland Telegraph Station. I know that was years ago, but we were wondering . . .'

'Never seen it myself,' McTaggart broke in, 'but I heard about it, and I seen what it done.'

'Will you tell us?' the boy asked, his interest a surprise even to himself.

The old man laughed, since this had been his intention all along. 'Was the third summer I was here, twenty-nine year ago now. A stinkin' dry summer it was, like the one before and the one before that. Not in all the time that I been here have I gone through anythin' like those years. I had days – sometimes four, maybe five on end – when I couldn't open the door of the hut. The dust filled me mouth like flour, fine as flour, then turned thick as dough. I wore a rag mask to breathe. Even lyin' there waitin' for sleep. I had chickens then and I lost the lot.

Just dropped dead. I seen crows fall dead out of a clear sky. It was that third summer, in the bad dry, that this bird came.

'Back then the telegraph station was still operatin' out at Eucla. It's a ruin now, but back then it was servicin' the last of the cattle properties. All gone now, they are. The last of them threw in the towel years ago. The operator at that time was a young fella named Willis. Snowy Willis, they called him, on account of his white hair, but his proper name was John. I'd see Snowy regular. I had a car then, an old Dodge, and every Wednesday I'd go up there 'cos Snowy couldn't leave the station unattended, and we'd yarn and have a drink and sometimes even play a hand of poker.

'This particular time – I'm talkin' high summer in that third bad year now – I couldn't get up there with the dry and the dust so thick, but when I did get to go, I knew straight off there was somethin' wrong. Somethin' was not right up there. I say this now like it was nothin', but that's not how it was.

'The station itself was a stone cottage built on a bit of a ridge. Every mornin' about nine. Snowy would go out and run up the flag, just a thing he had, the station being government owned and all, and every night, right on six, he'd go out again and drop it down. He was a funny fella like that. A real stickler for routine. But this particular day, about noon it was, as I came up over that ridge I seen the flag weren't flyin', so I drove up slow, feelin' a bit strange – unsettled like – and sure enough I seen Snowy lyin' face down in the doorway of the station. There was a covered verandah right along the front and he was lyin' hard up against the door.

'Soon as I got out I seen that Snowy was done for. He'd torn away part of his trousers and I could see he'd busted his leg somethin' terrible. The bone was stickin' out above the knee and the flesh was rotten. Stinkin'. And there was flies all over. He was alive, but only just. I got him up and got him into the station. He was talkin', he never stopped once, and I got him to walk me through the workin' of the telegraph so I could put out a call for help. I got through to the base in Esperance and they said they'd pass the call on, but nothin' came of it. Nothin' could have. By sundown the wind came up, and the dust, and that was the end of Snowy. Was three more days before a plane could get in, and he was gone by then. Poor fella. Well and truly gone.

'But he talked, like I said. Sometimes right through the night, as he was lyin' there – waitin' for that plane, or death, whichever was comin' first. Anyway, he told me about the bird.

'So far as I can tell, and this is the story of a dyin' man, remember – a man who's hallucinatin' and takin' fits of fever – he'd been workin' in the station when he heard this commotion outside. He had a cattle dog, like Blue here, but even older, see, and she was puttin' on a turn, barkin' and raisin' hell, which was peculiar, since nothin' ever happened out that way. It was always quiet, like, so Snowy went out to take a look and here was the dog down in the dust and above her this bird.

'Now, I remind you again that Snowy was slippin' away fast when he told me this. And he didn't tell it like I am neither. Not all in one hit. Not connected, like. He told it all over the place, like I said. Sometimes makin' sense, sometimes ravin'. This bird was huge, he said. Three, maybe four times bigger'n an eagle. And it's comin' down after his old dog, whackin' at her with its claws. Beatin' at her with its giant wings. Well, Snowy goes for the bird himself. He runs at it, see, but it turns on him, bowls him over, flattens him, and then it's gone. Leaves the dog and disappears. And that's how Snowy done his leg.

'He got himself back to the station but the door was blown shut and there was no way he could reach up, lift himself, like, to open it and get in. No way he could get to the telegraph or get help himself. I dunno how long he was there. From the condition of the wound, I reckon four days easy, maybe more. Snowy, he lost track.

'You might be thinkin' all this is just crazy talk. You might be thinkin' all this I'm sayin' is just the talk of some crazy man been too long in the bush, but here's the part I know for sure. The part that makes me believe it. Come dusk that first day, before the wind come up, I got Snowy settled the best I could and went out back to check on that dog. Well, there weren't no dog. Not nowhere. Now I know that dog had been with Snow a good six, maybe seven years. She was a beauty. Faithful. Like my Blue here. She was a big dog too. But there weren't no sign of her, and she didn't show up, neither, not in all the time I was there. So there's a few things, see. First, there's no way that dog up and walked away from Snow, not with him being crook. No way. Second, and this is what I truly believe, that bird come back. When I was in there tendin' to Snow, that thing come back and took that dog. Lifted her clear away. No ordinary bird done that. No eagle's big enough. Pickin' a carcass to bits on the ground, that's one thing – I seen eagles do that plenty – but there weren't no carcass there at all, see? That dog was taken. Picked up and taken. And whatever done that was some bird. That's what I say. Some real special bird.'

When he had finished there was a silence, until Muir said, 'So you never actually saw the bird yourself?'

'Nope.'

'And you don't even know the direction it took after that attack?'

'Nope.'

'Would you have any idea? I mean, where it could be nesting?'

'I heard one theory, but . . .'

'Yes?'

'Back in the '50s, they say the government was testin' bombs way up north. Atomic weapons, like. Now, I never seen this place meself, but they reckon there's stretches of desert up there, maybe two, three hundred k's square, that's all sealed off. All fenced off. Electric fences. Standin' maybe four or maybe five metres high. Could be that's where this bird come from. And what made it grow so big. Changed by these atomic rays, see?'

Muir rubbed his forehead. 'You're suggesting that it's not a natural species. Maybe a mutant?'

'I heard that, but . . .'

'Who from?' Mala interrupted, barely disguising her disbelief.

'There's the odd traveller comes through. Even way up here, but . . . ah . . . I reckon I talked enough for one night. I reckon it's time I hit the hay. So if youse don't mind . . .' At this he got up and returned to his hut, but the agate-eyed dog stayed beside Simon.

Mala and Muir exchanged glances.

'So,' he said, 'looks like we head north first thing tomorrow.'

'North? Whereabouts north?'

'Up around that old test site.'

Mala laughed. 'You don't believe that nuclear mutant thing, surely?'

'Not for a minute. The reports of sightings go back too far for that. Long before the atom was split. But if the area's been sealed off for years, there might be a chance our bird's up there. Hiding out.'

'What about the telegraph station? I thought we were supposed to be going there?'

'What's the point? You heard his story. The bird hasn't been seen anywhere around there for years. Besides, who wants to see a ruin?'

'I do.' She spoke with such determination that he was taken aback.

'Why? We're looking for the bird, not just where it's been seen, aren't we?'

Simon saw her hesitate before answering. He watched her think the words through before she spoke. 'Greg,' she said, 'don't you mean where it's rumoured to have been seen?'

Muir took a second or two to grasp her meaning. 'No, I meant what I said. Where it's been seen. I don't follow . . .'

Mala had been holding her coffee cup at chest height, taking the occasional sip. Now she lowered it slowly, looking at him hard. 'Greg,' she said, 'when are you going to accept the fact that there isn't any bird. I mean, you just heard McTaggart. He's a great guy, but he's loopy. And, besides, even he admits that he never saw the bird himself. I mean, Greg, we're supposed to be scientists. If we are, where's our evidence?'

Simon was beginning to enjoy himself. He liked to watch the fireworks between this pair. But he pulled his feet back quickly when Muir got up and began pacing around the fire in earnest. 'Mala,' Muir began, 'there are certain things that you just know. Certain things that defy scientific proof. And I know that bird is out there. I just . . .'

Mala's laugh cut him off. 'Are you listening to yourself? Did you hear what you just said? What bird are you talking about, exactly? I haven't seen any bird. I can't send Shane a whole pile of "just knowings" or "gut reactions" or "feelings in my bones", which is what you're going on about. And I can't photograph words, either – which is about all I've got. A whole pile of words. Yarns. Rumours. What else is there? A scrap of fabric that might have been ripped off a hang-glider's suit. Great. That would come up really well on the cover of *Rare Earth*, wouldn't it?'

He turned to look at her, his face lit from beneath by the firelight. 'I understand now,' he said. 'It was the photos of the sites that you wanted all the time, wasn't it? That's how come you want to go up to that telegraph station, isn't it? Because you're photographing every site where the bird is *supposed* to have appeared. The whaling station on Mondrain. And Hellfire Bay. That's your angle, isn't it? You're not doing a story on the bird at all, are you? You're just out to prove that it doesn't exist.'

'So? If it's the truth, what's the harm in that?'

'You can't do that. You can't . . .'

'Greg,' she said, leaning forward, 'don't try to tell me what I can or can't do. You might have once but, believe me, those days are long gone. Do you understand?'

He stopped his pacing and nodded. 'Yes, Mala, I understand. And I'm sure that Simon here does too, by now. But there's something that you need to understand: "the truth", as you call it, isn't something that comes in a nice tidy package, all done up in plastic like a loaf of sliced bread. There are as many truths as there are people in this world. People who sincerely . . .'

But Mala would not let him finish. 'No more,' she said, getting to her feet and emptying her coffee into the fire. 'I'm too tired to listen to another one of your sermons. The point is, bird or no bird, I'm not going anywhere near a nuclear test site, even if it has been closed for forty years. OK?'

Muir was standing quite still, staring into the fire. 'Up to you,' he said softly. 'But life has funny ways of . . .'

'Good,' she said, cutting him off for the second time. 'So tomorrow we head up to the telegraph station. That should complete the sighting locations. All right?'

'All right,' he said.

'I'm turning in. Simon, you get your beauty sleep. I might need a hand setting up the cameras tomorrow. Goodnight.'

Both Muir and Simon muttered and then a silence fell. Muir continued to pace and the boy stared into the fire. But the agate-eyed dog got up and nuzzled at the boy's leg and was not satisfied even when Simon reached down to pat its head or stroke its ear. Still it prodded his shin with its nose; butted his thigh with its bony forehead. 'What?' the boy whispered, looking down. 'What is it?'

As if in answer the dog backed away – whining softly – inviting the boy to follow, which he did, since Muir had seen and heard none of this, taken up with his own thoughts as he usually was.

The dog headed towards McTaggart's hut. A dim light was visible through the hessian-covered windows and Simon realised that the animal was leading him to its master. He hesitated, not wanting to follow. It was dark outside the glowing firelight and the miner had made it clear that he'd had enough of company for the night.

'No,' he whispered to the dog. 'Go on home. Go on.'

The dog fawned and pawed at the earth, all the while yelping in a strange inviting way, until the boy was forced to kneel and stroke it, thinking that was all it wanted after all. When this was done, and Simon licked and slobbered over, it still would not go.

'Get,' he said. 'Go on. You're old enough and ugly enough to find your own way back. Blind or not.'

'He might be old an' ugly,' a voice called from the darkness, 'but he sure ain't blind.'

The boy peered into the shadows and saw McTaggart seated on a chair outside his hut, a glass in one hand and a bottle in the other.

'Sorry,' Simon said. 'It was like the dog was wanting me to follow.'

'I reckon he was. He ain't stupid. Because I was wantin' you to come, see.'

At this the dog left the boy to sit at the feet of its master.

'There,' McTaggart said.

Simon stood in the yard, not knowing whether he was listening to a drunken madman or whether he should step up and sit beside him, answering the call of a friend.

'I have to go back,' he muttered. 'We're leaving early in the morning.'

'Leavin'? Where youse headin' for?'

The boy looked down and shuffled in the dust. He pulled the lock of hair over his forehead. 'Not sure,' he said.

'Not sure?'

'She wants to go to the telegraph station but he wants to head north. To that old test site. They were arguing about it.'

'Who won?'

Simon cocked his head to one side, trying to see the man more clearly. 'Couldn't tell,' he lied.

'They arguin' about this Wazo bird? Is that it?'

The boy nodded.

'Who's right, you reckon?'

'I don't know . . .' he was about to add, 'or care', but he stopped himself before the words were spoken and kicked the dust again. He couldn't say that. Deep down, he knew that he had cared for some time.

'So, you stayin' down there wearin' out shoe leather, or you comin' up here to sit with me?'

Simon came and sat down as he was asked, but would not take a drink. 'Never touch the stuff,' he said, which was true.

McTaggart took a long drink himself. 'Youse ever heard of this Atman? The one who gets the flowers?'

Nothing could have prepared the boy for this. 'The camel man?'

'Him.'

'I saw him on the beach, down near Esperance.'

'Once, maybe twice a year, he comes up this way.'

'What? To collect flowers?'

'Sure he collects flowers.'

'I don't follow . . .' the boy said.

'There's flowers and there's flowers, ain't there? So why would anyone come up here lookin' for flowers?'

'I heard that he collects rare species. That no-one knows where he finds them.'

McTaggart nodded. 'That's true. And where these flowers come from, there might be other things. Strange things, like.'

The boy turned towards him, trying to see his face in the dark, trying to read what was in his eyes. 'Strange things?'

The man raised his glass slowly, sipped from it and lowered it again. 'Could be that bird,' he said. 'Ya never know.'

'Why didn't you tell them? Why didn't you tell the others?'

'Dunno. Maybe I was just tired, or maybe it was seein' you there, your head bent crooked like that – lookin' and listenin' like you're part bird yourself – and I seen how the dog come over to ya, natural like, and I thought maybe we should talk later. Just the two of us. About this bird.'

'You have seen it then? Is that what you're saying?'

McTaggart laughed. 'Son, I might be a lotta things, but I ain't no liar. No, I never seen that bird, but I did see somethin'. Just for a second. No more . . . That day up at the telegraph station when I went out to check on Snowy's dog, I told youse all that she was gone. She was a big dog, I said, right? But she was gone. That bird had taken her, I reckon, leaving nothin' but some blood on the dust. 'Cept when I turned to look – just turned around, like, to check the animal weren't behind me, hidin', there was this feather. No bigger'n' me finger . . .' and he paused to hold up the little finger of his right hand, as if he were drinking tea from the daintiest cup. 'No bigger'n that, driftin' at me feet. Blue, it was, blue like I never seen before. Not even in the bluest o' sapphires. Not even in them. I took another look around – why I couldn't say, maybe to check if the bird was still there, maybe to see if there were more of these feathers – but it was then this wind come up, not much, but enough, and I seen that feather rise up outta that dust and disappear. Up it went, into the sun. I tried, but I couldn't follow it. I couldn't see it. Blinded I was, by that sun. And just like that, it was gone . . .' he lifted his glass and drank again, reliving the memory.

The boy waited, knowing there was more.

'Then one day – six or seven year ago – that Atman comes in here. Ah, he'd been here plenty before that. Two, sometimes three times a year, as I said, ever since I come here. But this particular day I was out here workin' on somethin' in the yard and I seen him comin'. Seen this dust cloud, way over to the west, and I thought, this ain't no twister – they never blow in from there. Nor'east, always. So I watched. And little by little I seen his camels come up on the horizon, and then him walkin' beside, and after a while he comes in here to get water. Give them camels a drink, like. Turnin' south to Esperance he was. All loaded up with flowers. Hangin' down from these trusses on them camels' backs. All upside down, to dry, like. Anyway, we got to talkin'. He don't drink whisky neither. Like you. But he'll talk. Not a lot. Never tells where he's been exacdy, but then I reckon that's his business. He don't go askin' how many stones I dug that week either. Or their colour or size. But this was the first time I seen the direction he come from, see? I never seen that before. Sometimes I'm underground, down the shaft. Sometimes I crawl out of the cot of a mornin' and he's here in the yard. Turned up durin' the night, like a spook.' He drank again.

The boy waited.

'Now the reason I'm tellin' ya this is that when the time come for him to go, when them camels were all watered and rested, I come out to see him off. I give him some of me special balm. Keeps ya safe from the sun, see? And the desert wind. All the elements, like. Make it meself, I do, from these desert plants. I pack it in me empty tobacco tins. Don't worry, I'll see ya get some before ya go.

'But this day, with this Atman leavin', I took him out a tin and while I was handin' it to him me eye catches on this feather caught in the flowers, see? Blue it was. That same blue as the one I seen at the telegraph station all them years ago. Bigger, this one was. Maybe ten, fifteen centimetres long. But the same colour. Now this Atman, he sees me lookin' and he takes the tin of me balm with one hand, and he lifts that feather out from those flowers with the other and slides it down inside his shirt. I seen him but I didn't say nothin'. If he's been around that bird, it ain't nothin' to do with me. I don't want nothin' to do with that bird. If there's anythin' I wanted, it's his camels. If I had them, I could go out west meself. Not after no flowers. Nor no bird. There's sapphires out there. That's what I'd be after, if I had them camels. But if you're wantin' to know – you, personally, are wantin' to know where I, personally, think that bird is, well, there's your answer. See?'

'West?' the boy asked, still uncertain.

'A day, maybe two from here, due west, there's these ranges. Mean, granite country they say it is. You come up from the south? You seen those granite islands off the coast there? They was mountains once. Ten, maybe twenty million years ago, before the sea come up. That's the same as the ones out there. Old country. Lonely country. Nobody goes there, hardly . . .'

The boy stroked the dog's head and got up. 'I should call it a day,' he said.

'Wait.' McTaggart disappeared into the hut to return with a tobacco tin. 'This here's me balm. Just a bit on your face. For protection . . .'

Simon took the tin, mumbled his thanks, then stepped out into the yard. 'Due west?' he called, turning.

'I ain't been there,' McTaggart answered, 'but I reckon that's the way.'

The boy nodded, smiling to himself, and in the morning, as he shouldered his pack and left them all sleeping, he smiled again. A curious secret smile, even by his own reckoning.

With the sun no more than a line of rose along the east, Simon was walking into darkness. He was not happy about that. He did not like the dark. Yet he felt the warmth of the sun's rising; first striking the back of his neck, then his arms, then his legs and, in time, penetrating his pack to warm his body.

He thought about the things that he carried. The things he had been given. The backpack itself was from the counsellors, Graham and Burwood, who hardly thought of him now, he imagined. There was the bone-handled knife from the old woman at Esperance. There was the tin of desert balm from McTaggart. 'For protection' he had said, and the boy laughed, thinking of magic elixirs and snake bite antidotes and other mumbo jumbo cures.

There was the water canteen Mala had given him at Mississippi, which he now remembered that he had not filled, but the morning was still fresh and he supposed that he would come across a creek or pool before the full force of the day's heat struck. There was also the compass from Greg Muir. So precise. So ordered. So sure of itself – like Muir himself, with all his answers, and he laughed again.

He walked without particular purpose, except to be free of the others – a course which came to him naturally. When they woke up they would find him gone. He doubted that they would come after him. Why should they? What was he to them, after all? Nothing but a liability. Yet there was some reason, some secret thing lying sleeping in his mind, that led him to take this way – to head west – that he could make little sense of. To have a definite sense of direction was strange to him, but he walked on, heading always for those rolling granite ridges that formed the horizon, guessing that between them would lie stony gullies or hollow pockets or wooded valleys to conceal his course. If anyone should choose to come after him. To haul him back . . .

Soon the harsh morning sun struck his neck and he felt the heat shoot like pokers into his head. He turned sideways to the distant hills, trying to evaluate the distance he had to travel before reaching them, but the haze off the sand and the soft edges of the ridges made this impossible. He put his hand to his neck, feeling the burning there, and regretted that he had no hat, no protection. He did not think of the balm.

The best thing to do is keep going, he thought. To keep putting one foot ahead of the other. I have made the break. If I go back now Muir will have a piece of me. Then Mala would have a piece of Muir. He couldn't stand the thought of that. Although it made him laugh, he hated their stupid bickering. He had hated it in his own parents. Always bickering. Especially about his condition, as they called it. His eye. 'A child with his condition,' one would say, 'should not be allowed . . .' or 'A boy in his condition ought not to be . . .' Which meant that he was always watched – to the point where he felt like a specimen, something trapped or caged.

Towards the end of the sand there were gibbers. Flat red rocks the size of a dollar and thin as a biscuit. He amused himself stooping to pick them up in stacks, like gambling chips, then shying them away towards the hills. Some skipped once or twice on the orange sand and slithered to a standstill; others shattered in a spray of dust.

After the gibbers the sand changed from orange to rust-red, as if there was some mineral exuding from below, iron perhaps, and the surface softened until Simon was aware that there was moisture beneath. He squatted at the edge of steamy soaks, which shimmered in the heat, reflecting iridescent oils, the colours he had seen on the blue-black backs of bush-flies, and he cocked his head, as was his way, to watch minute carnivorous plants, viciously barbed and fanged, and sticky pads and webs that oozed sickly sweet honey-dew and the odd black ant engulfed within and struggling. But there was nothing that he could drink – would allow himself to drink – so he determined to put his thirst behind him and pushed on.

This was not easy. Although he could see the beginnings of the ridges not so far away, the sand and gibber surface over which he had made such good time was now thick with steely tufts of needle-sharp spinifex grass, so that every footfall was a burst of pain. Like being stung by wasps, which had happened to him once when he had charged into a nest from his wrong side – his blind side – and had no idea what caused the sudden burning that struck and struck and struck at his face, piercing his skin, even attempting to penetrate the glassy hardness of his false eye. Or so the doctor had said as he wiped the poison from its surface.

The spinifex lay between him and the distant ridges and before he had covered a hundred metres he could hardly bear to put his boot down, knowing that the moment he did the barbs would penetrate his jeans and stab his flesh, making his eye smart, making him yelp and cry out.

But he would not go back, and when he finally stood upon rock, he recognised it as the same granite that he had seen on Mondrain, the hills, grey hemispheres as smooth as those of the Recherche Archipelago, worn and weathered from the same primordial range, ancient as the earth itself, but here as yet uncovered by ice or tide and still half-buried in the earth.

He found a grey-leafed tree that offered some shade and sat down beneath it. He unlaced his boots and took them off, then his socks, which were filled with prickles and burrs, then he lay back and rolled up his jeans, examining his legs. They were running with blood and the flies swooped on him so fast that he got up, put on his boots and walked on.

Within an hour he had entered a shallow valley, but the heat reflected from the granite slabs was so intense that he looked desperately for water, hoping that in some hollow beneath the rocks there might be a pool or a spring. He found none and cursed himself for having left camp without first filling the canteen.

At midday, which he judged by the dazzling sun directly above, he came upon a dank and muddy soak, but he would not drink from it, considering it too foul – yet as he left he heard the rapid whirr of tiny wings and looked behind to see a pair of grey-banded finches suddenly appear to settle and sip the moisture from the imprint of his boot. This was the water he had scorned, and although this time he was tempted to drop to his knees and lap it up, still he went on, ever hopeful of some pure and bubbling stream.

There was none, though he looked all afternoon.

At dusk, when he could take no more and had no idea where he was and had long forgotten what his intentions were in going anywhere at all, he threw down his pack and stretched out in the cooling shade of an overhanging rock. He took off his boots and socks and placed them neatly beside him. He took off his shirt and bloodied jeans and rolled them all into a pillow and lay back on the granite.

He felt the swollen size of his tongue and the creeping of the flies over the black scabs that the heat had already formed on his legs.

He lay there until darkness fell and a creeping fear came over him. 'What's the point?' he said to himself. 'I hope that I die. I hope I go to sleep and die.'

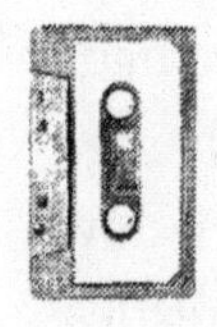

22 October

My dear Shane, I'm not quite sure what to report this evening, whether I should be angry about what happened today, or guilty, or even happy! I think I mentioned in my last tape that we were heading towards a sapphire mine – well, we found it without any trouble and McTaggart, the old codger who works the place, invited us to camp there for the night. He was quite a character, one of those loners who love to tell stories – when they get an audience, that is! He, of course, had his story about the Wazo and according to him, it's thought to be a mutant, created by the nuclear testing in this area some years ago. He was also able to tell us what happened out at the telegraph station, since he was a mate of the linesman and had found him after the supposed attack by the Wazo. I won't go into the details now – I've got the conversation recorded on a different tape – but he was another one who spoke like a 'true believer', yet when it came down to it, he was still only speculating about what happened to his friend – he didn't have any actual proof, and he hadn't seen the Wazo himself.

Even though we could have gone to the test site or the telegraph station next – Greg and I had an argument over that – we didn't head for either. In fact, we've had to drop the assignment all together for the time being, I'm afraid. We've been hiking west, trying to track down Simon. A few days ago I thought he was getting restless, I think I even mentioned it to you. I should have said something to him then.

When we woke up this morning he'd gone. At first we didn't realise what he was up to. His sleeping bag was lying in the long grass as though he had just crawled out of a cocoon, so we simply assumed he'd gone for a walk, maybe to the toilet. But when he still hadn't returned after half an hour we started to get concerned. We soon realised that the rest of his gear, his pack and all, were gone as well. Even though the obvious explanation was that he had taken off for good, we hesitated when we saw he hadn't raided the food boxes and probably hadn't even filled his canteen as there was no evidence of moisture on the ground around the water bottles. We couldn't understand what he was intending to do.

It was hard to tell how many hours start he had on us, whether he'd been walking all night or had just left. McTaggart was no help, but at least he confirmed that the footprints we saw had to be Simon's. They were heading west. Why would he go west? There's nothing out there. What sense was there in putting his life at risk, just to get away from us?

I must admit, I was angry. First at Greg, for bringing

Simon and not looking after him better, and then at Simon, for not saying anything to me. I thought he and I were getting on well – maybe that friendliness was just an act on his part.

I felt like saying to Greg, 'You're the expert tracker. He's your responsibility. You go after him while I get on with my work,' but I knew Simon was in danger out there by himself, without tempting fate by having all three of us separate. You might survive thirty days in this desert without food, or thirty hours before exposure gets you, but it could only take three hours to die from dehydration.

Greg said he didn't want to wait to see if Simon would come back with his tail between his legs, saying he was sorry. Since he's silly enough to take off like that, by himself, we couldn't assume that he would have the sense to turn back. Greg reckoned it was going to be hard enough to track him in this terrain anyway, but if he decided to be devious, we could easily pass within a couple of metres of him and not know it. We had to go and get him, and we had to leave right away.

We couldn't take the station-wagon off-road, so we had to organise our backpacks for the trek. When Greg saw me packing my cameras he had the gall to say that I should leave them behind because they'd weigh me down. I explained that as the car wasn't being locked or hidden so if Simon returned he'd be able to get to food and water, I wasn't going to leave my expensive gear for anyone who might pass to help themselves. Anyway, I'm carrying them – and I've never slowed Greg down before.

It took us almost an hour to pull camp, pack the car and get ourselves ready.

Looking back at this morning, I realise that Greg and I worked together automatically. As we walked, Greg was watching keenly for Simon's tracks while I kept note of our direction on the map. But at the time my mind was ticking over, you know how it does, and all my anger towards Greg came spilling out.

I had a go at him about Simon. I said that this was my expedition, my work, and I'd invited him because of his skills. I'd assumed that when he brought Simon along he knew what he was doing, that he would make sure the kid was a useful part of the team. But I hadn't seen him doing much to help Simon – in fact, I think I've done more for Simon than Greg has. Like the other day, when we were bogged, Greg was so self-righteous. Now, because of Greg, the silly kid has ended up putting us all at risk.

Shane, I know you've never met Greg, but over the years you've heard enough about him to know that he's not easily shaken, although if something stirs him up he gets very passionate. When I'm upset I just talk and it's hard to stop me, but Greg, he has difficulty finding words in that kind of situation.

Still, while I was saying what was on my mind, I brought up the fact that he keeps on disappearing when he could be spending time with Simon. He said he took time out to write up his journal – and to meditate! I could hardly believe him!

Keeping a journal I can understand, but meditating . . .

I don't know what you think of meditation, Shane, but I know what happened to my mother in India. Those leaders who claimed to have gained great knowledge from meditation and who taught the scriptures were the same ones who claimed my mother was defiled by marrying a European, so they ostracised her and threatened her life. What sort of 'enlightenment' is that, I ask you? As I mentioned before, I think that stuff is all superstition. How could a scientist like Greg believe in those myths? It's as silly as me believing in St George and the Dragon. They're just stories that lead to ignorance. Science is knowledge based on *fact*. The Wazo is no different, and the fact is it simply does not exist.

Greg seemed floored by all this and mumbled some accusation about me seeing the world through my own confining lens.

But that was this morning and I think we were both relieved when we finally stopped arguing. Fortunately, we were able to follow definite signs of Simon's passage. Greg was remarkable the way he could see where Simon's boot had crushed the spinifex, where he had pissed among the granite hills, and when he saw birds take to the air he knew Simon was about two hours' walk ahead of us. But the thing that pleased me most was to see the boy's prints in the wet sand of a soak.

If we could only understand where he's going, what he's heading for, then maybe we could cut him off. We have to catch up with him soon or he could dehydrate and die. At least I can record tonight that Simon's still alive and moving.

Goodnight, Shane. I hope I have better news next tape.

Simon did not die. He slept. And as he slept, he dreamed.

In his dream he was in some other time and some other place. India or the vision of Arabia he had seen in the movies, where there were camels with crimson tassels hanging from their backs. He saw himself in this place, but not himself, since he, Simon, was observing a boy such as himself walking on a pathway of orange sand that was bordered either side by fields of tall yellow grass. The sky was clear and midday blue. As the boy walked, his attention was caught by a movement, high up to his left. He had to turn bodily and lift his head to see what had caused this since, against his dreaming-will, he saw that the boy in his dream had no sight in his left eye and there, as in a painting or a photograph, an eagle circled.

This bird was huge. Bigger than any in the boy's Field Guide which he produced from nowhere and consulted. But the bird had no colour. It was visible to the eye only as a shimmering.

Fascinated, he watched as it levelled out then swooped to the earth. He was curious to see what it was hunting and ran to where it had landed. He stopped in the middle of the field, panting, trying to catch his breath, and suddenly the bird was there. It stood taller than the grass – as tall as the boy's dreaming self – and he froze as it turned to stare at him. Now he saw that its eyes were coloured. Golden, the colour of honey. Then it spread its wings and flew off.

The boy followed, running, panting again as he tried to

keep up. But he could not. He could not look up and look ahead at the same time and he fell in the grass, frustrated, as the bird vanished over the horizon. When he lifted his head this was not, in fact, a horizon at all. It was a frame. An edge. The non-developed edge of a photograph. So it was quite logical that the tall yellow grass should part and a dark-haired woman holding a camera should appear.

This woman knelt beside the boy and held out a water canteen. 'This is a gift,' she said. When he took the canteen and put it to his lips he found that it was empty and the woman had gone.

He stood and looked about. The grass was so thick and so tall that he could see nothing except the space of the midday sky overhead. Once again it was quite logical that the grass should part and a man with a map should appear.

This man knelt down beside the boy and held out a compass. 'This is a gift,' he said.

When the boy took the compass and tried to read it he found that he could not and the man had gone.

'Now I'll never find the bird,' the boy cried. 'Never. Since I do not know where I am myself.'

'Nor who you are,' called the boy who watched from the edge of the frame, after which he vanished, as had the shimmering eagle, leaving the dreamer to wander and fall again and again until he could not get up, and lay down and closed his eye to sleep the sleep of death – only to be woken by a grey dawn and the sound of tiny bells.

Simon woke and listened. These were not bells. These were parrots. The same rainbow-coloured parrots that had flocked above the circle of sticks in the dunes. At once he scrambled up and dragged on his clothes in the likelihood that he was not alone.

Then the parrots came. Exactly as they had before. They streamed down the stony valley. They were gorgeous to him. All that was life and freedom. All that he could be, but was not. Shaking off the last of his dreaming, he cursed at them as they swept down the valley, until the flash of their rainbow colours was lost and the sound of their bell-calls fell silent.

He was sorry then and picked up his backpack and went after them, calling, 'Wait!' and 'Come back!' and 'Stop!', which he knew to be stupid but he had no choice in this and, curiously, *knew* that he had no choice. Knew that he was being called, or *driven*, or made to do this, which was against everything that he had ever believed in, everything that he had ever wanted for himself, but he would not have stopped even if there had been a choice.

Because he knew Atman was there.

Which he was, seated in a semi-circle of boulders, leaning back against one, the birds spread before him, their rainbow feathers broad as a garment. When he saw the boy he raised his ancient head and greeted him with honeyed eyes.

'You are Simon,' he said and as he spoke the rainbow parrots lifted as a flock and wheeled through the valley, their bell-song echoing after.

The boy followed them with his eye. When he looked back, the old man stood before him, as fantastic in reality as any dream.

'I am Atman,' he said. 'I have been waiting.'

'Waiting?'

'The camels and me.'

'You know my name.'

'I have my ways,' the man smiled.

The boy flicked the hair from his face and saw that the boulders the man had been seated against were in fact camels, their dun-coloured humps camouflaging them among the stones. 'I see,' he said.

'And would see better,' Atman replied, 'would see everything better – if you had used your gifts.'

'Gifts?' the boy repeated stupidly, transfixed by the golden gaze of the man.

'You were given gifts for this journey. And on it.'

The boy was amazed. 'Who told you?' he asked. 'McTaggart?' The miner was the only person he could think of who might have spoken to the man.

'Not McTaggart. But he gave you a gift, didn't he?'

'What?'

'He gave you a tin of his balm?'

'Yes, but . . .'

'That was a gift. A gift you have refused to use.'

'It's some awful slop in a tobacco tin. He makes it out of leaves. Squashes up some desert plants and . . .'

'Show me.'

The boy slipped his backpack to the ground without question. He had no choice but to obey. That was the way it was.

'And who gave you that pack?' Atman asked.

'These guys I knew. Back home . . . These guys who looked after me . . .' As soon as the words were spoken he thought, What am I saying? What am I thinking? Home? What home? But he dropped to his knees and found the tin of balm.

'So the pack was a gift too?'

'I guess . . .'

'No. Guesses are unfair to the giver. And to the receiver. I will ask again. Was the pack a gift too?'

The boy's hand was extended, holding out the tin of balm. It was clear that it would not be considered, not even looked at, before the question was answered. He lifted his head, challenging the man with his single eye as he had done so many times to so many others. But the old man's gaze did not waver. He waited – wiser, stronger – until the boy begrudgingly admitted. 'Yes. It was a gift.'

'Did you thank them for it?'

'I guess not.'

'Guessing again. A pity. Such a useful gift, a pack such as that, for a traveller such as yourself. For one on the way. And there were other gifts?'

'A knife. Some old lady gave to . . .'

'What knife? Show me.'

Once more the boy knelt and rummaged through the pack. The bone-handled knife was at the bottom. He found it and held it out. This time the man's acceptance was immediate; his response instantaneous. With one movement the knife was prised open, its sharp and brilliant blade revealed, and then with another, and another – too fast for protest, too quickly to duck away – the boy's concealing forelock was grabbed and cut off.

The action had been so fast that Simon could not believe it had happened. Yet there was the crescent of yellow hair glinting among the stones at his feet. 'Holy . . .' he muttered, but the curse was never finished as the old man spoke. 'That's better,' he said, stepping back, admiring his handiwork. 'Much better. Now you can face the world. Look out and up at the same time. And I can apply the balm. Here . . .'

He took the tin and opened it, twisting its lid deftly as only the experienced could. Before Simon could recoil the old man's fingers were pressed into the balm and he was anointing the boy's forehead, his burning face, and all the heat of the desert was gone.

Simon did not move. The knife and the tin were replaced in his hand and his fingers closed over and around them, then the old man bent down and, with slow and deliberate movements, picked up the lock of hair and placed it in the boy's other hand, saying as he did, 'This is yours. Dispose of it wisely.' Without comment or complaint, Simon knelt and put the knife and the tin away in his pack and pressed the hair into the safety of his shirt pocket against his chest. After this he stood up – still reeling a little and not entirely himself.

'Sit down,' the old man said, pointing towards the shoulder of a rock. 'Sit down. There are things that I need to tell you. Now that you are ready.'

Simon had no idea what he was talking about, yet he did as he was told and sat. The old man himself sat opposite, cross-legged and facing him direcdy. 'Look up,' he said. 'I know what you are hiding. I know about your eye.'

At this the boy did look up. He looked up sharply, stunned that such a raw and tender wound had been so cruelly opened. 'There was nothing to look at,' he said, 'until you cut the hair away.'

'It was time for it to go and you know it. To hide behind your hair was childish. Worse, cowardly. Besides, who were you deceiving? Nobody. Least of all yourself.'

Simon did not reply. In the last of his defiance he could only glare, turning his head to one side to concentrate his vision, his hurt, as had always been his way. Atman simply smiled and would not withdraw his gaze. 'You look silly,' he said. 'Foolish.' The boy felt deep tears forming, which the old man understood. 'I am not saying that you are foolish to be angry,' he said. 'I believe that you have every right. You have lost an eye – and since we have been speaking of gifts, it is only fair to admit that sight is one of life's greatest gifts. One of the greatest of the senses. One of the key means by which we read our world. It is true that to be blind would be a great loss. But you are not blind. You can read the world and all its colours. Better yet, having one eye only, the body has compensated. For you there is the greater possibility of looking not only out, but in – and the gift of inward seeing is the greatest gift of all. Yet such a gift is not always recognised. Not always valued. Nor accepted. Now tell me, what other gifts have you been given? I am certain there are more.'

'A canteen,' the boy answered, daring to trust his voice. 'And a compass.'

The old man nodded and smiled. 'Yes,' he said as though he had expected as much. 'What have you done with those?'

'Nothing. There was no water worth drinking. And I knew where I was going.'

'You are dry now.'

'Yes. But where there are birds there will be water.'

'I see. And you know where you are going?'

'Yes. Due west.'

'Which is . . . ?'

That way.' He pointed in the direction that he had been travelling.

'You are certain?'

'I was just going. If I got somewhere – found something – that would be a . . .'

'A bonus?'

'Yes.' The boy was starting to feel his old cockiness returning.

But the man was far from finished. 'Bullshit,' he said.

'What's bullshit?'

'Your talk. How many gifts have you been given?'

'What's that got to do with anything?'

'Answer me.'

'I don't know. A pack. A knife. Some ointment. A water canteen. A compass . . .'

'You were given nothing else?'

'No.' It was imperative to the boy that he be right. That he win. 'No,' he said again.

'Then is taking the same as giving?'

'I never took anything. Ever. I'm not a thief.'

'You took a feather. A blue feather from a circle of sticks. Inside the stones . . .'

Simon's head jerked up. 'How do you know?'

'How I know doesn't matter. Not now. But answer this. Was that feather left there by chance?'

'I saw it and I took it. So what?'

'Was it yours to take?'

'Who cares? It was just a lousy feather. I saw it and I took it. I already told you that. Maybe I thought it was a gift . . .' He meant this as a joke and immediately he regretted it, knowing that whatever game he had been playing with this old man – whatever this stupid contest was about – he had suddenly lost.

But Atman was not out to score. He smiled and said, 'Yes, it was a gift.'

'From you? That was supposed to be a gift from you?'

'No. Not from me.'

Simon laughed outright. He couldn't help himself. 'What's all this about?' he demanded. 'How can some stupid feather be a gift? Don't tell me I talk bullshit.' He slipped from the boulder and shouldered his pack. All he wanted was to get away. To run. But the old man's next words stopped him dead. 'So,' he said, 'you know where to find water, do you?'

Simon turned back, his answer at the ready. 'I already told you how.'

'That is true. But where are the birds? I can't see any. Or hear them.'

'You must think that I'm blind. I saw the parrots here. And heard them too. So there must be water. Plenty of it.'

The old man lowered himself from the rock. 'What if I told you that the parrots travelled with me? What if I told you that they were sustained by me? My flock. My cover.'

'So you carry their water?' he asked, his voice sharp with cynicism. 'Enough for all of them?'

'No. I don't carry it. How would I carry it? I lead them to it. How else would they fly this far? Not over desert.'

Now Simon began to understand. If there was water, it was in some secret place. Some hidden place where he might not find it. Some place only this Atman knew. Some place that he led his birds to. His tongue seemed to thicken and swell at the thought. 'If there's water, I'll find it. Or else I'll go back.'

'Go back?' The old man folded his arms and waited, his eyes alive with expectation.

'To McTaggart. I'll go back to the mine. And then to Esperance. Anywhere out of here.'

Atman nodded, a model of patience. 'So, if you don't find water here, you will re-cross the desert? Still without water. Is that it? Because if it is, you will die.'

The boy knew that he had made a fool of himself and he was silent.

'But there is a solution. A way out that only you can provide.'

'What?'

'That you ask. That you simply ask for help.'

'I never ask for help. Ever.'

'Then you will die.'

Simon knew that this was true. It was not about the water, though he would die without it. No. It was about admitting. About owning up that he could not always make it alone. That he did need help. To ask, at least. He lifted his hand to pull the hair forward, shook his head when he realised it was gone, then stepped forward, saying, 'Atman,' – it was the first time he had spoken the name – 'I need to fill my canteen. Will you show me where I can find water?'

The old man's face shone. 'I will,' he said. 'I have been waiting.' And he walked slowly away, shuffled almost, the boy noticed, in the direction of the camels.

Where the hell is he going? Simon wondered, since he had expected Atman to head off through the meandering valleys to some distant pool, but no sooner had the man entered the boulders, hardly a stone's throw from where the two had talked, than he stopped and called, 'It's here. Right next to you.'

Simon did not move. 'What?' he asked, passing between the rocks to see. 'Where?'

At his feet was a shallow pool. On its slimy surface floated the membranous bodies of long-dead insects. He could never consider this as water, if that was what the old man had expected. Which it was.

'Get your canteen,' Atman said.

'That's worse than those soaks in the desert,' the boy protested, shaking his head in disgust. 'I can't drink that. Nobody could.'

'My parrots have. My camels have.'

'They're animals. Not humans. No human would drink that. No way.'

'I have,' the old man replied with a wry smile. 'So what does that make me?'

It was a question Simon had already considered. Confused again, and incapable of responding with the usual smart quip, he looked down to the pool, watching slow, dull bubbles form and burst.

'You see,' the old man said, 'I can do no more than show you. I can't make you do anything. Your choice is a hard one, that's true, though simple too, since the outcome is plain enough. Drink and live. Refuse and die. It's up to you.'

Which was the truth. Unless there was another pool, that fantasy of sweet, clear water, somewhere secret, down the valley, hidden in the hills. Unless the old man was tricking him. Forcing him to act against his will. But what for? No reason that Simon could think of. He understood then that there *was* no choice. Not in reality. As the old man said, either he drank this muck or he would die. Well, most likely die . . . And though he had toyed with death in his dream the night before, he returned at once to get the canteen from his pack.

When he came back Atman was seated, waiting, his face wan and tired, as if some strength were draining from him. Simon noticed, but did not stop. He removed the lid from the canteen and pressed it into the ooze, allowing fluid to trickle in. Not much, but enough to moisten his tongue, ease the burning in his throat, dull the aching in his stomach. Only then did he pause to check that he was being watched – to acknowledge his need, once, in that single glance from that single eye – then he drank.

He grimaced and wiped his mouth with the back of his hand. Without being asked he knelt and pressed the lid into the pool again. He repeated the process three times, as if to prove that neither the first time, nor the second, had been an obligation – a humbling – but an act of will. Not easy, yet necessary. But when he bent a fourth time the old man called, 'No more. Let that settle. Fill the canteen, not your stomach, or else you will be sick.' Simon took the advice without question, filling lid after lid and pouring the contents time after time into the belly of the canteen. While he did, kneeling at the pool, the old man seated himself on a flat rock, folded his legs beneath as before – though his back seemed not so straight, his chin not so high – and spoke quietly to the boy.

'Will you go on now that you have water?'

'Yes.'

'Still heading west?'

'Yes.'

'But how will you tell? How will you know which way is west?'

Simon thought a moment. 'By the sun,' he answered, and hoped that he could.

Atman shook his head. 'What if there is no sun? What if the rains come – which they will, any day now. There will be no sun at all.'

'The rains?' the boy repeated, glancing up as if they were coming right then.

'Worse, if you are going west, the valleys narrow to crevasses and the crevasses to labyrinths. Labyrinths so dark that to miss a turning is to lose your way. You think that I am lying?'

If the boy appeared to be smiling, it was not his intent. 'No,' he assured the old man. 'Go on.'

'If you should make it through – if the labyrinths do not claim you – then there is the Curtain Stone. And after that the Needle's Eye. Darker still. Darker than any starless night.'

Now Simon was afraid, yet there was something about this man that he could not shake off. Something right. Something strong. 'The Curtain Stone?' he repeated, his voice suddenly fearful. 'The Needle's Eye? What are they? And why should I . . .?'

'Not "Why *should* I?", but "Why *will* I?" That is the question. The question only you can answer. Although, if you remember, you have the compass – a very important gift. Unused, I believe?'

Simon said nothing, which was answer enough.

'This compass, it has a cord strung through it, to hang around your neck?'

How could anyone know that, the boy wondered, save for Greg Muir who had given the thing to him? But he answered, 'Yes,' since it was true.

'Good. That leaves your hands free.'

'My hands free? What for?'

'To hold a light.'

'A light?'

'A compass is no good in the dark.'

'But I haven't got a light. Not even . . .'

Atman smiled. 'Whether we have two eyes or one, we are all blind without light. So that is my gift. Matches. A candle. The gift of light.'

'I don't even have to go that way. I'll go around. Some other . . .'

'No. There is no other way.'

Simon clenched his fists in frustration. 'No other way to *where*? You keep talking as if you know where I'm going when I don't even know myself. I'm just going. Somewhere. Anywhere. That's what I do. OK?' He turned to leave, convincing himself that at last he could go, yet turning once to call, as a parting volley, 'So I don't need any stupid candle.'

But the old man knew that they were far from finished. 'Only a fool would decline such a gift,' he said. 'Particularly if he is frightened of the dark . . .'

Simon's head resounded with the words, with the truth behind them, and he turned again, slowly, his face set, emotionless – or so he hoped – and answered, 'All right. I'll take it. But I don't know why.' This was a lie, so he added for good measure, to cover his fear, 'Since I'll never use it.' He followed the old man back to the camels and accepted the gift, and some damper, and some cheese – mouldy, it's true – thanked him and was ready to go when Atman put a withered hand on his arm, turning him gently about.

'What?' the boy asked.

'I know where you are going.' The old man's voice was trembling, but the boy was tired of the game, and only wanted to leave.

'I told you a hundred times,' he said, 'you couldn't. I don't even know . . .'

'You are on the way to the bird. I know it and you know it too.'

Simon laughed. This was all too silly. 'No,' he said. 'You got that wrong. It's not me who's after the bird. It's the others. The others back at McTaggart's. The bird's their thing. Sorry . . .'

'Really?'

What could he say in reply? Once he would have walked away – gone anywhere, any place – sure that he was right. That everyone else was wrong. Even to blame. But now he could be certain of nothing. Nothing at all. Although, somewhere in his heart – or his head, which worried him all the more – he knew that he *was* going after the bird. If he made it through the valleys and that labyrinth and that

Curtain Stone and into that Eye – that Needle's Eye – he *might* see it; *might* find it . . . But he said no more and left, without turning back.

At least, not then.

He chewed on the cheese and damper as he followed the course of the valleys. He felt good. Free, as he always did when he ran. He heard himself whistling and felt fine about that too. But when the gentle curvature of the hills grew steeper, the passage between them narrower, the shadows longer and deeper, a sense of foreboding fell on him, silencing him, reducing him, and he touched the compass at his neck, pressed his hand against the matches and candle snug in the back pocket of his jeans. And when he reached what he knew to be the labyrinth, he was glad of these gifts. Very glad that they were there.

The labyrinth was a dark place. A place where the hills crowded together, their cold granite faces close, breathlessly close, crushed one against the other in a suffocating confusion of infinite alleys. Everywhere was darkness, even though it was not yet midday. Atman was right, he told himself. I could get lost here. He reached for the compass again and, holding it higher, towards a shaft of sunlight, he read for the first time, unaided, the direction of true north. From that, even if he was one-eyed, to find due west was nothing.

But reading a direction and following it were two different things. The fact was that if the compass said, 'Go this way', the granite walls did not. And where there was an opening, a fracture or a crevasse, it could lead to the east or the south. Or first this way and then another, looping and winding back upon itself until all sense of direction was lost. If only I was above, thought the boy. If only I could fly, and look down, the way out would be so clear. He thought of the bird, and how it might fly over, seeing the way so well. If there was such a bird. Or even a way. But he went on, stopping to read and re-read his direction from the compass and learning all the while to back up and turn and check again and again, until he noticed the path widening, the sunlight increasing, the sheer cliffs reducing, then he knew that he was almost out.

When at last he had come through he found himself in an open valley. To the west was a range of rugged hills, higher than those he had just passed between, and he guessed – no, knew – that over there, somewhere, were the Curtain Stone and the Needle's Eye. Maybe even the bird. And he sat down to take a good look at the place.

He could cross the valley in an hour, maybe less. Only then, if he felt like it, need he make up his mind to go on at all. If he didn't want to – and here he touched his pocket to be certain that the matches and candles were still there – then he could turn back altogether. After all, he reminded himself, he had made it on his own a hundred times before, a thousand times, so why worry now? He was his own boss, despite what Atman had said.

With that self-assurance he got up and set out across the valley, whistling as he went.

At first he did not use the compass, since the way seemed so clear, so open, but even here, when he got down to it, there were boulders that appeared as pebbles from above and dense undergrowth that appeared as shrubbery from a distance, and he might have lost his way in going around or between, if he had not forced himself to stop after every detour to re-read his true direction. This tested his patience but he did it, and in an hour he stopped to see where he had come from. He smiled and patted the compass that hung against his chest. 'OK,' he said aloud. 'OK.' But when he turned and looked ahead, there was only the bald surface of a mountain of granite. He stepped back to reconsider. The peaks on either side were higher and steeper than the one before him.

He tightened the straps on his pack – a process that was now second nature to him – and tested the grip of his boot against the granite. 'Good,' he said then, leaning towards the rock, he began the climb.

The surface was weathered and pitted and he made fast progress. Two or three times he paused to look down, congratulating himself on how far he had come, how high he had climbed, and so easily. When he looked up he saw that the face grew steadily steeper, yet it was not threatening, and about two hundred metres further was a ridge that formed a summit. Beyond that, he hoped, was something . . . that Curtain Stone. Whatever . . . and he climbed on.

But not to the summit.

The surface suddenly fell away. When he reached out there was a void, a chasm. He stood up, balancing as best he could. He looked to the south and to the north. There seemed to be no end to this, as if a great slice of the surface stone had torn away, separating itself from the base rock to grind agonisingly down, rock against rock, aeons ago. He could not go on. It was impossible. There was no way he could bridge that divide – no way that he could climb or leap across – and he sat down to gauge the extent of this barrier of nothingness. That's what it was, a barrier of air. No more, no less. If he was a bird . . .

He descended on his backside, cursing and muttering to himself.

Once on the ground he turned to the north to find the gap still there, its presence disguised by boulder and scrub, and then to the south, where the result was the same. Now he understood. He was there and had been all along. Had been climbing the thing. Crawling all over it. This *was* the Curtain Stone: a sheet of fabric-thin granite that had slipped from the main stone ages before. The

Needle's Eye was beneath it, he was certain, if he could find the way in.

Since it was the nearest he entered the gap at the south end. It was gloomy, the air fetid. He was far from happy, but sunlight filtered from above and he went on until the chasm narrowed to no more than a crack – a fault line in the greater rock – and he could go no further. OK, he thought, still certain. I'll try the north.

From the first – once he had negotiated the secret of its entrance – the north entry seemed to welcome him.

Seemed to open to him. There was so much space, so much width and height, so much air and light, that he could not imagine why it should be called the Needle's Eye. An army could pass though this. As Atman would know. Still, he reassured himself, this was right. This was the way.

Which it was, but not then. Not the way, for this boy, right then.

As in the south, the chasm narrowed. Not so much as to make him feel trapped. Not threateningly close. A camel could still pass. But the gap swung sharply to the right, to the west, and as it did the view was changed. The rock closed over above him and the sunlight was lost. Before him was a vault of utter darkness with no end in sight. This was it. At last the Needle's Eye. But he could not enter. Not even with the candlelight, he knew. It was too terrible. Asking too much – too fucking much – and he hitched his pack and turned away.

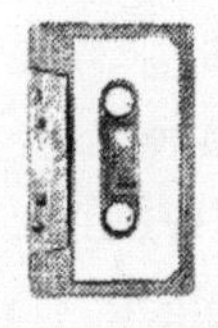

23 October

Shane, I'm afraid it's not good news. We still haven't caught up with Simon and Greg is very anxious – so am I. Anyway, Greg wanted to make a small recce to see if we could take a short cut to make some ground on him. It's not that we haven't managed to close some of the gap, but not enough, obviously. So I've found some shade and I'm stretched out for ten minutes till he gets back.

I can't stop thinking about all that's happened over the last couple of days. If I didn't know better, Simon's speed and direction would indicate that he knew where he was going, whereas, right at this moment, it feels as though I'm the one who's lost, especially in light of what Greg said to me yesterday, and what happened late this morning.

We were travelling fairly well, concentrating on the terrain, staying quiet, when we heard a peculiar sound. We went to investigate and as we drew closer we could hear something dragging in the sand, bushes being bashed, and a soft thud. We rounded a boulder and came across a monitor, about two metres long, twisting and turning and clawing at something black in its mouth. At first we thought it was wrestling with the prey it had just seized, but since the meal was already disappearing down its gullet, it didn't make sense that the lizard should be working so hard. When it stopped writhing for a moment, we could see black feathers sticking out of its mouth. Greg realised that a bird must be stuck in its neck, and the monitor was choking. Its contortions and flailings on the ground were from pain. Next thing I knew, Greg dropped his pack and shepherded the monitor into a corner against the granite walls. He edged closer and closer, and when the lizard lay still, he pounced. In that split second it twisted away and Greg barely grabbed hold of its neck. It fought back, trying to escape, and its claws tore into Greg's arms. Greg grabbed again, this time getting a better hold. Then he made a mistake: he lifted it up too quickly, without having turned the creature completely so that its back would be facing him. This meant its hind legs were able to come up and claw his stomach.

I managed to grab the thing's tail and together we laid it on the ground. Greg pinned its body with his knee and slid a hand over its eyes. With Greg holding it still like this, I was able to release the tail and get at its mouth. I tell you, Shane, the sight was gruesome. A huge crow was jammed sideways in its neck. I had to stretch open the monitor's mouth and at the same time grab hold of a very dead crow. But the bird was stuck solid and covered in slimy gastric juices, so I found it hard to get a good grip. I was afraid of tearing the lizard's throat if I just pulled, so I had to wriggle the carcass, twist and coax it with all my strength. Once I finally dislodged it, it slithered out easily. And all the time, even though Greg had blood dripping down his arms and soaking his shirt, he never stopped soothing and talking to the monster.

When you realise that Greg continually battles to stop monitors raiding his sanctuary for eggs and preying on his injured birds, I think what he did was pretty special. He did confess he hesitated a moment and thought, 'Good, one less monitor to contend with'.

He was hurt badly, especially his left arm, so I got him to sit while I cleaned and covered the scratches. That brought me in close to him, you know, close enough to feel his breath in my hair. So I asked him, 'Do you care for anyone as much as you care for your birds and animals?' And just like that he replied, 'Yes, you'. He said he hadn't told me that before because he thought I was no longer interested, that I wanted to be alone. I said he had it all wrong, that I didn't want to be alone, that's why I left. I had felt very alone with him, because he wouldn't talk about himself. And when he said how he didn't tell me things for fear of ridicule, I realised that I had always seen him as the untouchable tough bushman who never gets hurt.

It's as though I've been so busy with my life that it's somehow got in the way and I've forgotten to consider how everything I do has an effect on the people around me – just like in all ecosystems, I guess.

So, I bent forward and kissed him. Since then the fog seems to be lifting, the tension between us is clearing and maybe, for the first time on this trip, I will be able to feel comfortable with him.

But we can't relax yet, we still have to find Simon – before it's too late.

I'll keep you posted Shane.

Simon re-crossed the valley and passed once more through the labyrinth without so much as a second thought for the way he had left behind. When he had made the decision to run, that's how it was. Not to think of looking back. Still, there were strategies – ploys and evasions – that needed some consideration. There was Atman. How to avoid him? He might even see Mala and Greg Muir, but he doubted it. He guessed that they would have gone on to the telegraph station or the nuclear site, rather than waiting at McTaggart's. He laughed just to think of it, taking off as he had. He remembered his counsellors, always chasing after him, always on the hunt. Still, he watched his step. He negotiated his path.

The first of his obstacles was Atman, who could be somewhere there, in the valley at the end of the labyrinth.

Simon stepped out into the sunlight, his eye squinting to adjust to the sudden brightness. Now, he thought, how to get around; how to avoid being seen? He had no intention of encountering the old man and explaining his return. Why should he? He never had before. Not to anyone. As for the so-called 'gifts', since they were his, why did he need to justify their use? They were given to him, not to some old man.

He took in the terrain with a sweep of the eye and decided to keep to the higher ground. Atman would stay down in the valley. If the old man was travelling at all, he would be slow. He looked tired, or sick, and he had those camels. The boy was confident that he could skirt around him if he took to the ridges, if he climbed. He liked doing that. He liked the heights, looking down as he had on the cliffs at Mondrain and when he had climbed the Curtain Rock.

So he went up, following the contours of the ridges, leaning inwards towards the rock, steadying himself with one arm against the granite face, the other outstretched for balance, conscious all the while that if he fell he would die. He would roll over and over and over until his skull cracked against a rock and that would be the end. The precariousness of it all excited him. The razor's edge.

Now he could take a bird's eye view, as he had dreamed. Now he could look down on the landscape that he had travelled before; see the winding pathway through the valleys that had led him to Atman, to that labyrinth and beyond. If he looked up, and out – which he could, now that his hair was cut – he could see the desert stretching away to the east. Somewhere out there, he knew, was McTaggart's hut and that agate-eyed dog. More than once he stopped and sat down to catch his breath or eat the little that remained of the damper – the mouldy cheese was long gone – and he wondered what he would do when he got there. Would he stay, maybe one night, or go on? Turn south maybe, and get back to Esperance? Better still, ask McTaggart to take him, now that he had learned to ask, or been taught.

As for Atman, Simon did not see him. If he was in one of the valleys he was not visible. Nor were his camels or his birds. Maybe he was blocked from sight by a hill, the shadow in a valley, or maybe – which was most likely – the boy was swinging well away from the route he had taken when he had made his way in. Following the ridges was shorter, faster – not needing to dodge outcrops of boulders or clumps of rugged scrub – and yet he could maintain his direction with no more than a glance at the compass on his chest. Progress was fast, his spirits high, until he caught a movement, a shift in the landscape. He stopped and looked. There, beneath him, he saw two figures. He knew at once they were his minders, Mala and Greg Muir, who had come to take him back, for certain.

He pressed himself against the face of the rock but he need not have bothered. Even from where he stood, maybe fifty metres above them, he could see that they had bigger problems than him. For whatever reason, Muir was struggling with an enormous lizard that thrashed about beneath him. He saw the creature claw at the man's arms, lift its hind legs to tear at his stomach, and the boy clambered down the rock to watch from the safety of a clump of boulders at its base. Only then did he understand. The lizard was in trouble. Something – a crow, he saw – was wedged in its jaws, choking it, and Muir was attempting to hold the thing while Mala, crouched in front of it, was pulling the bird out.

Simon watched, fascinated. He had never seen Muir behave like this; never seen him demonstrate such strength, such steadiness. Muir was obviously determined to save the animal, irrespective of the cost to himself. And throughout it all, he made no sound. But this was not the half of the boy's amazement. Never had he seen the two of them – woman and man – work together as a team. They did not speak to each other, either to demand or command. Each seemed to predict the other's needs, the other's actions, as if by instinct. He saw also that Mala wrestled with the slimy black mass of feathers in the lizard's jaws without disgust, shoving her hands into the slavering mouth without a trace of fear. More than that. He saw that she lifted her head again and again to interpret the expression on the man's face, the tensions of his body, and Simon was struck by the understanding there – her admiration of him – a thing the boy had never noticed, never realised, before.

When the bird was freed and the lizard released, Mala talked to Muir. Reassuring, Simon supposed, soothing, then she leaned forward to kiss him. And he returned her kiss.

Embarrassed, the boy crouched lower. He felt like an intruder. His head was reeling with all that he had seen: not just these last few minutes, but well before that – his experiences since he had left McTaggart. Something was not running to schedule . . . if there ever had been a schedule in his running.

He realised that this was the second time he had stopped when he had no need to. Once with Atman, and now again to see Mala and Greg. Even thinking of them in such terms, by their first names, came as a surprise to him. Why had he stopped? That was what he wanted to know. Or was it the reverse? Why – no, *how* – had they managed to stop him? That was the problem. That was what was new . . .

He got to his knees and peered between the boulders again. Mala and Greg had their backs to him. They had moved away towards a clump of rocks where she was making a fire. Boiling the billy. Greg was seated beside her, watching her. Talking. She unzipped her backpack and removed the tea mugs. Greg's pack was nearer; he must have tossed it aside when he went after the lizard. His water canteen had slipped out and lay beside it. There was an apple too, the green of its skin vivid against the orange dust.

Simon felt a sudden longing to slip out and take them. To taste clean water. To feel the crispness of a bite of the apple. But a sudden shame came over him, a feeling that was strange to him. To think that he could have done that, could have stolen from them. They had done him no harm. No harm at all. They had only come after him because they cared. Nothing else made sense. Not like his counsellors, who got paid to chase after him and a hundred other kids like him. Who could hardly tell the difference between one kid and another. But not this pair. They had gone out of their way to find him. They must have. They had been so determined to keep going north, to the telegraph station or that test site. Maybe they even liked him. They liked each other, that much was obvious. Now, at least.

He crept back, to think. To decide whether to go on, or to stand and own up. To stop wasting their time. To put them out of their misery.

But he could not face them. He was not ready for that. It was too soon. Too much. Yet he couldn't just walk away. Couldn't just run, as he would have once. Before Atman . . .

He remembered the gifts and what the old man had told him. What he had learned from him – although it was hard to admit – of the value of both receiving and giving. Yet he had given these people nothing but trouble and he felt the shame well up inside him again and could not, for the life of him, shake it off. He touched the compass that hung about his neck. That had seen him through. As had the canteen. There was the backpack from Graham and Burwood and McTaggart's balm. Even the silly little knife, hardly more than an ornament, had served a purpose. A purpose that he would never have had the courage to put it to. There were the matches. The candle from Atman. Unused as yet, but not without value. Not if there was dark, real dark. And there was the feather – that blue feather – which was more of a promise than a gift.

From whom, and of what, he could not tell. Not for certain, though he had his suspicions.

He put his hand to the pocket of his shirt to check that the feather was still there and felt the outline of its shaft. But something else as well. Something fuller. Cushioning. It was the lock of his hair. He took it out and ran it between his fingers. He had not realised how long it really was. How far it had fallen across his forehead. His eye. It seemed so stupid. As the old man had said, who did he think he was fooling? He sighed as he twisted it between his fingers. For so long it had been his hideaway. A tell-tale sign of his childhood, now that he allowed himself to think of it. That's what it was. Or had been. His stupid refusal to face the world. His cowardice. And he threw it down on to the red dust, hardly noticing as the hot desert wind carried it away.

Once more he glanced back and, satisfied that he had not been seen, hitched his pack and made his way to the ridges. For once his destination was certain. He would retrace his path, keeping to the heights, bypass the labyrinth, cross the open valley and return to the northern end of the Curtain Stone. There, he knew, he must face the Needle's Eye. His fear rose up at the thought of the darkness of the place. The closeness. But he would not go back. Not now. And he hurried on, more and more determined that this was a fear he must face. A horror he must overcome. Not simply for his own sake, but for those who had helped him. Believed in him.

In time, when he stood before the entrance to that place, he was more certain. He put his hand to his chest and felt the feather there, its promise. He reached for the candle, lit it, then stepped forward into the dark that would be the making of him: the death of him, yet the life of him. The future that he was yet to know.

23 October

Hey, I'm recording this from the back of a camel! No, Shane, I haven't gone completely mad – I *am* riding a camel, and I've been on it for a couple of hours.

Things started to happen not long after I recorded my last message. I was standing catching my breath after finally scrambling to the top of a steep hill, when out of nowhere came what sounded like a thousand bells. A great cloud of western rosellas wheeled and swooped past and came to a stop over in the next valley. They had settled in a clearing, some perching on rocks and others on the backs of three camels! I was amazed. As far as I knew parrots and camels don't have that sort of affinity. Greg and I went down to have a look and we realised the camels weren't wild, since they were haltered and hobbled. I recognised the Indian-style halters and knew they belonged to an old man I know, Atman.

I don't know if you remember, but I told you about Atman once before. He looks as though he comes from northern Pakistan or Afghanistan and he has that special smell of the desert. People seem to know very little about him, and the stories that circulate contradict each other. From what I can work out, he came to

Australia as a young boy and has been wandering the desert ever since. Years ago, before there were proper roads, he provided a kind of mobile supermarket for the miners. Recently I've seen him carting wild flowers for sale in Esperance. People say he pops up at the most unexpected times and places. A bit of a rare breed.

We found him lying in the shade of a boulder. At first glance I thought he was dead. He had flies crawling over his face, through his sparse white beard and the deep creases around his eyes. But he was only sleeping and with each breath his thick lips wobbled, making him look as vulnerable and innocent as a baby. We tried to wake him gently and when he opened his eyes he seemed frail, not at all like the spritely man I had met before. We had to help him sit up.

We introduced ourselves and were about to tell him of our search for Simon when he said he had been waiting for us! No, he said, Simon hadn't spoken of our coming but, yes, he had met and talked to him earlier this morning. He assured us that Simon was tired but well and had gone on to 'finish his business'.

Even though I still don't understand what he meant, the urgency to race after Simon disappeared. So we sat with Atman and boiled the billy. At first I thought he was making small talk when he asked if we'd had a good journey. Then he asked us if we'd learnt many things on our travels. Greg and I didn't quite know what to say. Atman looked at me, waiting for an answer. A strange shiver went down my spine and I felt his eyes cut right through me, yet his smile was soothing. He just went on talking, saying that the outback can teach many things to those who are looking. Then he said, 'You're looking for something, aren't you?'

I made some silly reply like, 'I'm always looking for something new – I'm a journalist.'

Ugh, just wait a second . . . that's better, my leg was getting pinched by the saddle.

I asked Atman about his health because the change in him had surprised me. He said it was just the effect of time on his body, 'part of the cycle of life', and I worried about what would happen to him when we left. If he has trouble sitting up, let alone walking, how will he look after himself? I talked with Greg about taking him back to town, perhaps to a doctor or a nursing home, somewhere he could be cared for. If we made sure he had enough food, we could get Simon and pick him up on the way back.

But Atman just laughed at my suggestion and said, 'Firstly, I don't need food. I am too tired to eat. Second, I'll not leave my camels and be imprisoned in a town. No, thank you.'

So what we have agreed, and why I'm riding this camel, is for Atman to help us find Simon. If he is still feeling weak then, he comes back with us to

McTaggart's place. Greg and I insisted on that. We couldn't leave him here alone.

Shane, something is happening up front. Looks to me like we've come to a dead-end. I think Atman might have made a mistake and brought us down the wrong track – I'd better sign off – bye for now.

Hi, Shane, back again! And I've got good news! We've finally reached Simon. Atman obviously did know his way and I'm not sure we would have found Simon without his help. For those two hours we were riding the camels, Atman led us through a maze of interlocking spurs until we arrived at the end of a valley, which appeared to be blocked by a sheer granite wall – that was the dead-end I spoke of. We dismounted then, settled the animals and walked the rest of the way to the wall. It went through my mind that this man must be crazy if he thought I was going to climb that, let alone having to help him over. But when we reached the rock face he turned left and skirted along the bottom until he found a narrow gap. The wall we had followed was actually a separate plate of granite that had fallen like a curtain in front of the mountain. We squeezed in behind it and tracked back some way towards the middle of the rock, until we turned into a long narrow canyon. The light of day barely reached us at the bottom and the floor seemed to have been swept clean. The only traces of life were fossils embedded in the sides. Shane, you know me, I love an adventure, but this was really eerie! Atman just kept pushing on until the light was cut completely as we went into a tunnel.

I felt as though we were entering a new world. We emerged from the base of another sheer wall that ringed the plain sweeping before us. It seemed like an ancient crater. Low, feathery scrub ran gently down towards a grove of trees, maybe four kilometres away. Atman said that he had never been able to find another way into this region, and he has been looking for over twenty years. We were still at the mouth of the tunnel when he pointed and said, 'Is that the boy you're looking for?' In the lee of some rocks, not ten metres away, Simon was curled up asleep.

Even though Atman had assured us that Simon was not in danger and would be found easily, we were very relieved to see him for ourselves. But, standing over him, I had a rush of mixed emotions, and I guessed Greg felt the same. The relief and happiness of finding him safe and well was rubbing against the knowledge that he had run away from us, that he had put us in danger as well as himself. I couldn't tell how he was going to react when he saw us. Would he feel he had been saved or that he'd lost?

As he sat up, groggy from sleep, I could see that he had changed. Dehydration had left him noticeably thinner, and the long flop of blond hair that had covered his glass eye was gone. Now we saw his face, his whole face.

I started talking, trying to ease the situation, asking how he was and showing that we cared for him. But he kept quiet, head down, and only grunted in response. Greg had stayed back a little. He reached into his pack and gave Simon a couple of muesli bars, which he wolfed down. That must have convinced him that we weren't going to tell him off. When he looked up, our eyes met and he gave me a brief, embarrassed smile, and said, 'It's good to see you both.'

I guess we'll spend the night here and start making our way back to McTaggart's tomorrow. Only then will we be able to reassess our situation and decide whether to continue our search for the Wazo. I'll let you know, of course!

Bye, Shane.

WHEN THE FOUR eventually met, as Simon supposed they would, he asked if he could be alone with Greg. Leaving Mala and Atman to rest, the two set out towards the grove of trees that formed the centre of the saucer-shaped crater. Here, they assumed, they might find water.

They walked together for the first time since they had left the well-trodden paths of the Deep River Sanctuary, a time that now seemed so long ago. When they entered the cover of the scrub, Simon could not bear the silence any longer and, stopping suddenly, he said, 'If I told you that I was sorry, would you believe me?'

Muir turned towards him. He put his hands on the boy's shoulders and drew him to him, as if he were a son. But Simon was too ashamed to lift his head. 'Yes, I'd believe you,' Muir assured him. 'But you must also believe that what's happened had to happen. I tried to warn you, back at Deep River, but I know that was not the time for you to listen. You needed to see for yourself.

Out here, away from everyone, you learn that it's the landscape itself that's your best teacher. The solitude. The space. The ways of the desert and the mountains and the heat. The elements that throw you back on yourself. That force you to look in. I know, Simon. I had to learn that way myself, although I was older. Oh, yes, much older. And more determined, more self-willed even than you.'

When they reached the trees they found a clear, deep pool among them, shaded and cooled beneath the foliage. Here Simon lowered his pack and, asking Greg to sit beside him, washed the wounds where the monitor had lacerated his arms and stomach, then dressed them with the balm that McTaggart had given him. After they had drunk from the pool and rested a while, they returned to the others by twilight, talking of their adventures as they walked.

When they had eaten, the four sat by the fire. Night fell, and with it a silence, a certain peace in being there, although each knew that there was so much unsaid.

It was Simon who disturbed the mood, stirring the embers until a pillar of sparks rose into the night sky like golden stars.

Out of the silence the old man said, 'Even the heavens have birds . . .' Then he lifted his hand to point beyond the vanishing sparks. 'The southern birds,' he said, his voice smooth as honey. 'The constellations. There is Grus, the crane; Tucana, the toucan; Pavo, the peacock in its glory; and Phoenix, the one who burns . . .' His hand swept the heavens as if he stroked each shimmering star. 'But for you,' he said, 'there is only one. The one that you search for, I know. Which seems so far, yet is so close. Closer than you think.'

'How close?' asked the boy.

The dying embers lit the old man's eyes. 'As close – as far – as life itself.' He lifted his hand again. 'That is Aquila,' he said. 'The constellation of the eagle. The stars are its body. Its wings are outstretched as it flies eternally through the light of the Milky Way. On its breast, at its heart, is Altair, silver blue, and brighter than the sun. That, my friends, is your lodestar, the guide that leads your way.'

Simon shook his head, not comprehending.

'The light from that star, the glow you see now, set out across space before the time of your birth. You are sixteen, I believe?'

'Almost,' the boy answered, no longer surprised that the old man knew.

'Then the light from that star which falls on you now is older than you. Sixteen and a half years that light has travelled, through total darkness, to shine on you. To it

– by it – you are not yet born. You still live, unborn, in your mother's waters. Your mother's womb.'

'So, if I was up there, I would not be born?'

'That is true. But you see, Simon, you are here. That is the reality. And yet, it is never too late to begin again. To claim life again.'

'How can I? There's no sense in that.'

'That depends on you. From the oldest time the eagle of Altair has offered the promise of life. This is known to every searcher of the stars. When the eagle grows old and mist clouds its eyes, it flies upward – through the heavens – to the sun. There its wings are burned and it plummets down into the waters of the earth, where its sight is renewed, its life begun again.'

'That doesn't make sense,' the boy said. 'No-one with any brains would believe that. It's just a myth. It's not real,' and he fixed his eye on Atman, challenging him.

But the old man was equal to it. 'So you say now. Yet I know that you believe in gifts . . .' his voice was steady, his look unwavering, '. . . and their value?'

A wave of rebellion swept over the boy and passed, just as suddenly. 'Yes,' he admitted.

'And you still have an unused gift, which holds promise.'

'Which gift?'

Atman smiled. 'So you have learned to ask. Good. The gift that's in your pocket. Against your heart.'

Simon lowered his head.

'Tell them, Simon. It's time. Let them see.'

Without hesitation the boy took the feather from his pocket and held it out, its midnight blue shining in the firelight.

The old man nodded and turned to the others, who stared, wide-eyed.

'Tell them what it is, Simon.'

'A feather. From the bird. Our big bird. I'm sure of it. I know.' He looked toward Atman and smiled. 'It is, isn't it?'

'It is. And tell them how you received it. How it was presented to you.'

'In the sand hills near Mala's cottage there was a kind of nest. Not a proper one like that sea eagle's we saw at Mondrain. It was a circle . . .' He gave up, incapable of explaining, leaving Mala and Greg astonished.

Now Atman turned to Mala. 'And you,' he said, 'You have one too. Smaller, though equally beautiful.' He said this with such confidence, such assurance, that she shook her head in utter confusion. 'Me? How could I . . . ?'

Atman smiled. 'As the boy has learned – the hard way, true, but to his credit – certain gifts are received without our knowledge. They may lie hidden, until the time is right. I believe that this may be so for you, Mala.'

She laughed when he said this. Partly from embarrassment, partly in denial. 'No-one has given me any gift. And certainly not a feather like that . . .' She pointed to the one in Simon's hand. 'If they had, believe me, I would have it plastered all over the front page of every magazine . . .'

But Atman raised his hand, cutting her off. 'You met a woman called Gwen in Esperance, I think. At the museum?'

'Yes, but . . .'

'And she told you of the Wazo?'

Again Mala laughed. This time there was a cynicism in her tone. Even anger. 'She was an old . . .' but she said no more, sensitive to the age of the man she was addressing.

Atman let this pass. 'But she gave something to you?' he persisted.

Now Mala hesitated. A knife,' she admitted. A little knife, that I gave to Simon.'

'We are not talking about Simon's gifts,' he reminded her gently. 'We are talking about yours. What else did she give you?'

Only the crackle of the fire broke the silence. 'Her story?' Mala offered, realising that this was a gift too.

'Yes,' Atman nodded. 'Story is indeed a gift. One of the greatest. By story we may learn of lives other than our own, and thus enrich or shape our own. But that is not the gift I mean. It is the gift of the bird itself. Its promise.'

'If you mean a feather, don't you think I would have said? With that as proof, wouldn't I have believed in it?'

'Now, perhaps, is the time for that belief. Now, perhaps

you are ready. Like the boy, might it not be that you too had things to lose? Attitudes to discard? New ways to open?'

To this she said nothing, although she knew that he was right.

'Open your bag,' the old man instructed. 'The bag where you carry your livelihood. If not your life. There, the pocket to the side. See what you will find.'

As if in a trance Mala reached for her camera case. She lifted it and, placing it on her lap, unzipped a tiny pocket on the outside, as she had been told. She reached in, searching a moment until, amazed, she looked up, holding in her fingers a downy feather. Smaller than the boy's, but blue as heaven, even by that light, and she shook her head. 'You knew this all the time?' she asked, incredulous.

'I did,' the old man admitted.

'And Gwen left it there for me?'

'She did.'

'But why? Why not just give it to me? Why not just supply me with the proof? Why put me through all this?'

'You misunderstand,' he said. 'It is not for her, or me, or anyone else to *prove* anything. Nor to *supply* you with anything. It is for life itself to supply and you – and you alone – to test, or prove, what life has offered. The choices, and their outcomes, are therefore yours, and live within you. If you will look. If you have the will. The courage.'

'What choices? What outcomes? And as for my will, I have always . . .'

But here Atman looked towards the sky again. 'The rains are coming. By tomorrow this place will be flooded. To stay here could mean your death. Or, depending, your life . . .'

At this Simon tilted his head to concentrate his vision upon the old man's face. 'Or life?' he repeated.

'Perhaps,' Atman answered, stirring the fire to avoid his gaze.

'What life?' Mala persisted, desperate to know. 'What sort of life is there here?'

Atman smiled, and said nothing.

Only then did Simon understand. 'The bird?'

'Here?' Mala whispered, and covered her mouth, as if she had suddenly discovered some dark and secret thing, long hidden or denied.

'It has to be,' the boy agreed. 'That is the life . . .'

Still the old man smiled and yet, behind his golden eyes, brighter than the firelight, there shone a truth – a wisdom – which both boy and woman clearly understood.

'Then we should find it, now,' the boy determined. 'Tomorrow, if it rains, we'll have to leave.'

'Greg?' Mala asked, turning to him, 'What do you think?'

'You should go, and soon, as Simon says,' he answered. 'But it's not for me.'

Simon and Mala were stunned and began to protest. After all, he had come this far and now, with their goal so near . . . But nothing would stir the man to change his mind, until at last he said, 'You go and don't let me stop you. There's another life, right here, that's more important to me,' and, getting to his feet, he crossed the fire to sit beside Atman, who welcomed his presence as if that, too, had been foreknown.

'Thank you,' the old man said. 'Thank you.' Turning once again to Mala and Simon, he said, 'Your friend has understood that my time is coming. There is so much that we might share, the two of us, as I am certain that he knows. But for you who have received the feather, the way is open to you. And should you choose to take it, then it is, indeed, your way.'

'Greg?' Mala asked again, but when he shook his head, she knew that he had made his choice. 'Simon?' she asked, 'Are you ready?'

When he nodded, the two prepared to leave.

24 October

It's a quarter to four in the morning, Shane, and I'm huddled under a rocky overhang sheltering from the rain, which is pelting down. The two men and Simon are still asleep. I've managed to encourage last night's smouldering ashes to reignite but even through my sleeping bag the granite feels hard and cold. This morning's reality.

This is all so different to the dream-like state I remember from yesterday. The four of us were safe and together, sitting around the campfire eating dinner. I felt so good, Shane. Greg was telling Simon stories of his rebellious days and some of the silly predicaments he found himself in.

Then, when Atman started talking, the mood changed. I remember distinctly because of my reaction – I thought, 'Now, what's this old man on about?' But the more he talked, the more he sounded like my grandmother when she told her stories, and the more it soothed me. The rhythms in his voice were like the rhythms of the tabla weaving behind a sacred chant. He talked about the heavens and the constellation of Aquila and the myth it represents. Such a simple story, but it had the power to fire me with excitement and curiosity. I was mesmerised!

After, he talked about the Wazo. He said that he knows it exists, that he has seen it and that it lives here in this range. He even showed us feathers as proof. It is nocturnal, as Greg had guessed back at Mondrain, so we would have a good chance of seeing it right then, at night while it's out hunting. And in the cliffs behind our camp, there's a nest. But the rains were coming and Atman said the crater would soon be flooded. That meant if we didn't leave by morning – that's today – we'd be trapped.

After weeks of searching and being so close to getting a real answer, I wouldn't give up the chance to see the bird for myself, the whole, real, bird.

Thinking back, I realise that my usual logic had disappeared and it was as though I was in another mind state. Yes, clouds were rolling across the sky, and I couldn't dispute Atman's assertion that we would be trapped by the rains. I didn't even consider coming back another time to search in the safety of daylight, with proper resources. I just had to go, immediately, and nothing was going to stop me. Five minutes later Simon and I were ready. Greg chose to stay with Atman.

Initially my night vision was good enough not to need the torch. The granite wasn't difficult to climb, its surface was clean and Simon and I could get away with scrambling most of the time. But as the cloud cover mounted we were forced to turn on the torches. That didn't affect me as I had a head-torch, but it slowed Simon down, with his bulky hand-torch.

I remember thinking, Shane, here I am a photographer close on the tail of my greatest discovery and I'm not going to be able to take a photograph of any worth in this light!

It must have been about eight o'clock and we hadn't been climbing long, when Simon indicated to me that he wanted to take another route. He was lagging behind and it looked easier for him. We were to meet again at the top of the climb. When I arrived there I sat and waited, and waited. He didn't come and I never saw his torchlight again. That sent my mind spinning even more. I had to search, and keep searching, until I found both Simon and the Wazo.

Time lost its meaning as I explored those cliffs. At some point I felt an impulse to climb the jagged peak that stood out in the distance. As always when travelling in the mountains, each time I thought I had reached the top I discovered there was a higher point further on. I had crossed over one rise and was continuing to another when my heart thumped. The peak I was aiming for suddenly looked familiar – its silhouette was very much like a bird, like the hunched body of a huge raptor.

Fortunately my torch was turned off. I kept low and crept along in silence for about forty metres until the rock sloped steeply to a ridge. I eased myself up to the edge and peered over the top. And there it was – the Wazo! I'm sure of it, Shane. The bird before me was as tall as a human being! Taller! Close to two metres. Its head and shoulders were pale, probably white, its body dark, and even in the pale moonlight, its plumage had a brilliance, a sheen. I turned away, only for a second, to get my camera, but as I did a spear of lightning cracked open the sky. It must have startled the bird because it leaned forward, spread its enormous wings and dived. Right over my head. As I watched it glide away I pointed the camera in its general direction and furiously clicked as fast as I could, hoping by some fluke that I would get a print. The great bird glided then swept around in an arc, as though it was searching for a more protected perch.

Just thinking about this sends gooseflesh all over me!

I scrambled down so fast! I had seen the direction the bird went, though I didn't know how far it had gone, nor whether it had landed again.

Then the rain started – soaking, driving rain – and visibility dropped to zero, but I was determined it was not going to stop me. I continued scrambling and climbing – for the life of me, I *was* going to see the Wazo and I had to find its nest.

Before I realised what was happening, the ridge I had been following petered out. I had come to the edge of a cliff. A step to my left was a sheer drop and on my right was a vertical wall. Go back and go up, I thought.

But wherever I tried climbing my feet just slipped, my rubber soles lost all traction in the rain.

Even now I don't understand what happened. I've always found when I'm walking or climbing that there are plenty of paths to choose from, but somehow last night, in the dark and the rain, the only way I could find kept leading me back, until I found myself at the bottom again, where our climb had started.

So, Shane, I have a hundred questions filling my head and my heart – was my experience reality or a dream? And which experience would be worth more, anyway? For now, until I can understand better what has happened, not only last night but this whole trip, I'll leave it as . . . a dream in my reality.

I can't articulate all those other questions at the moment; if I did I would feel obliged to have the answers.

I'll talk to you again soon.

At first Simon and Mala had climbed together, he allowing her to take the lead, lighting the way upward, as she had the freedom of her head torch. He made slower going, encumbered as he was with a hand-held light. But soon there came a time when he sensed that the direction she was taking was somehow her own, not his, and he let her move ahead, a little at a time, until he called, 'Mala, go on. I'll meet you at the top.'

He followed the lower ridges of the crater's edge, which were accessible and free of boulders, until the real bite of the climb became apparent and the going was more arduous, forcing him to search for a safer path. The growing darkness did not help, the clouds spreading and thickening, the moon and stars waning.

Then, as he reached upward, his torch fell from his grasp and tumbled end over end into the crater below. He stopped and took stock of his situation. He had not brought his pack, not the gifts it contained, not even the matches and candle that Atman had given him. Only the compass that hung around his neck. When he looked up towards the blackness of the cliffs silhouetted above, a sudden fear came over him: that old fear of the dark, of total loss of vision and, momentarily, he considered going back.

That moment passed. He lifted his head and turned to focus more clearly on what towered above. The cliffs were dark, that was true, and within that darkness he detected a deeper darkness, ominous slashes of black that he could not clearly define. Yet it was towards these that he felt drawn, though to get there, to climb up and over the rugged and trackless terrain between, was a challenge that he must be equal to. He checked the compass, holding it out to the ghost of a moon, and was reassured. Due west, the direction he had been told to take, that had never betrayed him. Satisfied that he was right, he braced himself for the climb.

The way that he had chosen was a nightmare from the beginning. Almost immediately he was forced to scramble over a wall of tumbled stones. Even when he had managed this, no path was evident, only a greater confusion of fallen rocks far bigger than himself. Each boulder was a feat of perseverance to overcome, yet there was always another beyond, and soon he stopped, disoriented.

He glanced down at the compass but the light was too dim to read its face and he let it fall against his chest. All about him was the suffocating darkness of the stones. He could make out nothing that might sign his direction and, partly in exasperation, partly to gasp the humid air, he threw his head back, looking up. Then he saw the stars. Not so many as there had been when he had sat below – when Atman had stroked them as if they were at his fingertips – but one was still bright. Altair. The heart of the eagle. His lodestar, he knew.

Revived, he set out again and the scene opened at once. Not ten metres before him was the lower edge of a slab of granite that had shattered and slithered down – like the Curtain Stone, he thought – to form a gently sloping ramp. He ran towards it, leapt onto it and leant forward to take the slope. The moment he did, the compass struck the stone. He stopped and straightened. The instrument had been a gift, he knew, but it was a nuisance to him now – and he had the lodestar – so he took it off his neck, wound its string about his fingers, knotted it tight, and slipped it into the pocket of his jeans. 'Right,' he muttered, going on.

When he reached the upper edge, hoping for clearance, the yawning cavern formed by the fallen stone was in front of him. This was the deeper darkness that he had seen from below. There must be a way around. There must be.

But there was not. The dark had no end – no north or south – and when he returned from searching to stand before it again, to stare into its depth, he trembled. 'Again?' he said aloud. 'Do I have to do this again?' He knew that he did. He knew that this was the only way, though it filled him with terror to enter that dark, that confinement.

Once more he mustered his courage and went on. Went in. The cavern seemed fathomless, its floor sloping upward without apparent end. Yet he knew that it must end, that it could be no bigger than the slice of fallen stone that he had just climbed. That only made sense. Was only reasonable.

But reason did not come into this. To his mind, to his fear, it was a hellish place.

He walked carefully, although the rock beneath him was clear of obstruction, and some light – not light really, more of a filtered gloom – did fall from behind, from the last glow of the moon, the fast-clouding starlight. Now there was no lodestar, no guide, and to go on was an act of faith. Faith in the knowledge that he was still right – still on the path – though to where, to what, exactly, he did not know. Instinctively he put his hand to his chest, assuring himself yet again. As he did, he felt the feather, firm against his heart. 'All right,' he said aloud into the darkness. 'All right.'

Then he saw the first of the sticks – at least, that's what he thought they were, stepping over them – but something made him look back. They were very white. Bleached almost, like driftwood. He looked ahead. There were others, littering the floor. Piles of them, in clusters of three or four, scattered as if they had been tossed there, one crossing the other; all different sizes, different shapes and thicknesses – some straight, some curved, not like sticks at all, nor dead branches – they were too uniform for branches. They were more like bones. Like rib bones. He knelt down, extending his hand to touch one. They *were* bones. Bleached bones. Smooth. Cold. Yet living once, still charged with the long-lost gift of life. He remembered the whitened bones at Mondrain. Huge, they were. Of whales, taken from the sea alive, killed by humans and discarded; dragged into a chasm of the rock then slaughtered. And these, when he looked, seeing more and more as his eye adjusted to the gloom, were much the same. Smaller, yet bones all the same. There was no complete skeleton to be seen, no real clue as to the type of creature; not even a skull. No, he reasoned, this was all that remained of something that had been dragged here – whether living or dead – and eaten, its flesh stripped from the bone. This place was the feeding ground of a predator. A carnivore. A big one. A very big one . . . And the bird itself, this Wazo, was just that. A flesh eater. Its prey human, if need be.

The realisation struck. A fear far greater than the dark. He was human. He was living bone and blood and flesh. And he had brought himself here. Followed some path – however strange – to here. To be stripped to the bone. To be dismembered. To die.

I'm crazy to stay, he thought. But to go back . . .

He lifted his head, turning to focus on the dark, the end. He hesitated, thinking. To have come this far, and not know, not see this thing, would make him a coward, would cheat him of knowledge that he now yearned to have. There was more to this than finding some giant bird. It was the *knowing*. Knowing that he had, just for once, been trusted. Been befriended – and allowed himself to be – and come through.

He went on. Nobody was chasing, nobody guiding. He had no compass, no lodestar. Simply himself. His trust in his own intuition. The knowledge that this was right.

Beyond the bones, the floor of the cavern rose steeply and he bent down, aware that the rock above grew closer and closer. Still, he remained calm. Even when he was forced to drop to his knees and crawl, he went on, hearing his shirt tear on the narrowing fissure, ripping his jeans on the unseen. Where he was going he did not know, but the bird was close. Though why it should be in here – how it could be, if it was so big – was beyond imagining.

He could not look up, nor turn his head. He was forced to look ahead. Straight ahead. Even his single eye was useless now – to try to focus was hopeless. There was only dark.

Then the light came. At first a single dull ray, then a beam, then a peculiar radiance that defied belief. But there it was. An opening. He had come to the end.

He reached up, feeling the night air on his fingers, the back of his hands. He pulled himself through: his head first, searching, wary, then his shoulders, his chest, his body, until he crouched on open rock at the summit. He looked up to the sky.

The moon had gone and with it the stars, lost behind the lowering cloud. Far off, to the west, glowers of lightning lit the night, casting down an eerie light. By this he saw the rocks about him, and a peak – or what seemed to be a peak – no more than a few paces away. He looked again, concentrating his vision. It was not rock, not like the others that lay about. It was more regular, more formed, more circular than them. And yet it was not. It was more constructed. That was the word. Like a nest. A gigantic nest. That's what it was – and from it, quite slowly, taking its time, the head of a bird emerged. The bird, he knew. As he stared it turned to him, eyeing him casually, neither alarmed nor threatening, as if it had been expecting him. Slowly, very slowly, he stood up. The bird did not move. He stepped forward, excited, cautious, and moved closer, so close that he could look down on it. It raised its head to look at him with an air of dignity, of assurance, accepting him as an equal. He stood still – awed, waiting.

The creature had the form of an eagle – something that he had known, somehow – but its colours were beyond his dreaming. The head was pure white, the collar feathers blue, the body dark, yet blue all the same: that deeper, richer blue of the feather that he carried. The colour of the night. And then, with the sound of the wind, there appeared another. Down from the sky it came, its wing-span huge, twice the boy's height, more, eight metres, maybe, from wing tip to wing tip – to alight on the side of the nest. A pair. He had found a pair.

Both watched him, silent, their heads cocked to one side, their golden eyes assessing him, until the bird on the nest shook itself, ruffling its shimmering feathers, catching the lightning, raising itself from the nest to join the other, its partner, on the side. And in the nest, as if for his view, the boy saw their eggs. Four, each marbled white. Placed like compass points, like the cardinal corners of the earth.

He stood away. He looked first to the birds and nodded – as if acknowledging their presence, their beauty – then he lifted his head to the night sky, calling aloud, 'I am Simon Meekam. And I will be. I will be . . . OK?'

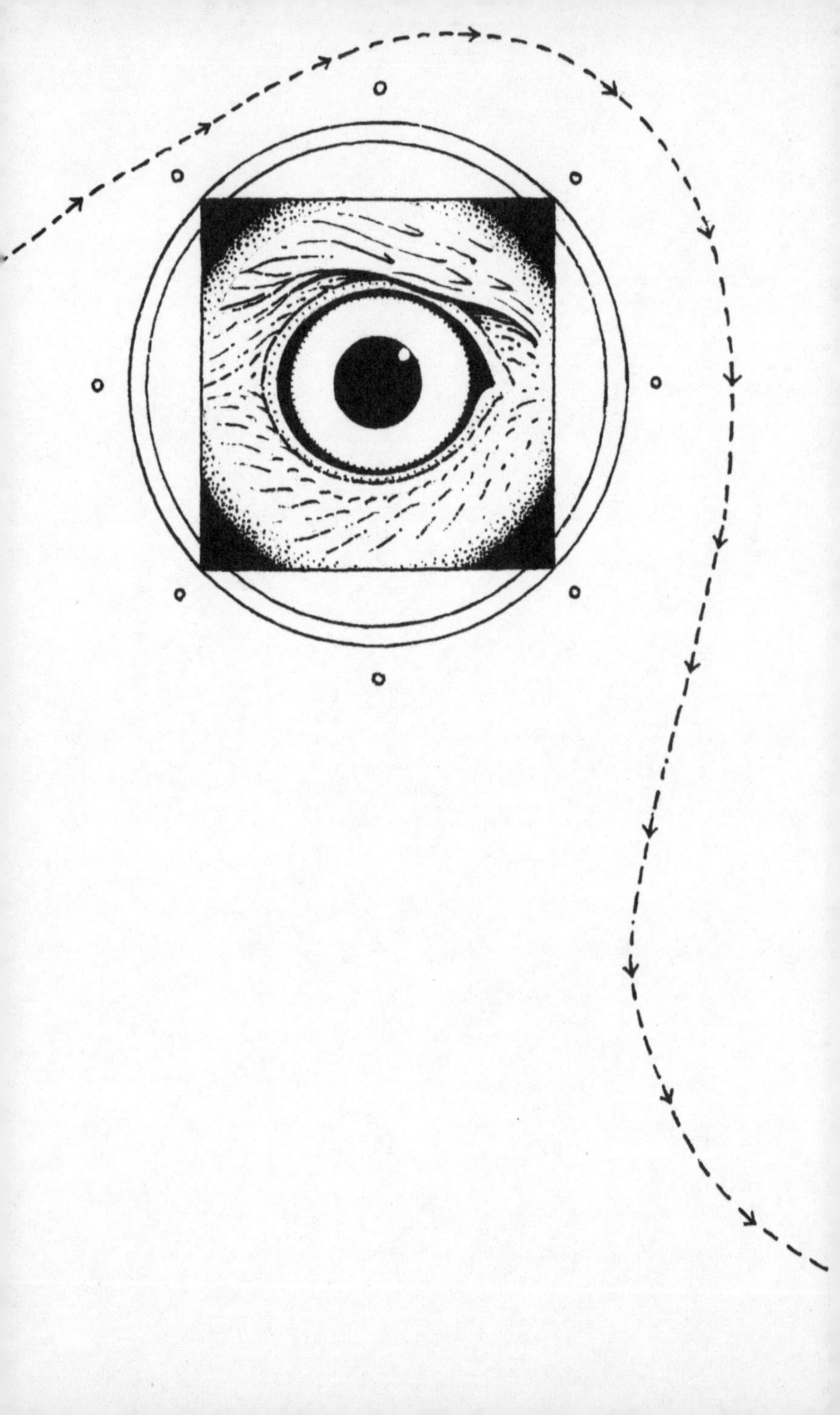

IN THE MORNING, when all had woken from a light and troubled sleep, Atman called them and asked that they sit by him, out of the rain beneath the rocky overhang where he had spent the night.

'You have been a great comfort to me,' he began, 'but now it is right that you leave me, that you should pass once more through the Needle's Eye and let me remain alone.' He lay back, placing his hand upon his stomach, strengthening himself before he went on. 'This body, human as it is, has been good to me, but now its time has come. I have a little to ask of you, before we part. There are my camels, hobbled, as you know, in the valley beyond the Eye. They will not have wandered far. Find them and take them to McTaggart. He needs them, and to leave them stray is not proper. They are alien to this land and have no place in it, not naturally. McTaggart is a good man and knows their ways, the dangers if they are released.

'In practicalities I have need of nothing, save some water and, with the rains, there is sufficient of that.' He paused to smile at his own poor joke. As he did, Mala knelt beside him.

'It would be wrong for us to leave you here. To do that would cost you your life. You told us that yourself, last night. There are three of us, all strong. We can manage you as far as McTaggart's, and after that we have a vehicle. We could take you back to Esperance, to the hospital.'

He would not listen. 'And have someone lock me up and nurse me? No. This is my place; here, within sight of the bird. Only here can I be myself. Be *with* myself. Here is my life. Only here can I pass over without fear.'

'Are you certain?' Greg asked, also kneeling beside him, and the old man gripped his hand in assurance. 'So I told you last night,' he answered. 'Would you expect me to take back my word? Come now, leave me to myself.'

Mala and Greg held him, then stood to leave, but as Simon approached the old man said, 'Let them go. You stay . . .'

Simon waited as he had been asked. When the others had gone Atman whispered, 'I believe that there is something you should tell me?'

A look of surprise crossed the boy's face. 'About the bird? I told you everything, when I told them.' He nodded in the direction of Mala and Greg.

'No, not about the bird. We have spoken enough of that. No. Something else.'

'What?' he asked, genuinely confused.

Atman drew himself up. 'Simon,' he said, 'out in the desert, I have brushed against thorns. At the time I might not know, but later I may find that one of them has broken off in my flesh. Broken off and festered there, secretly releasing its poison beneath the skin. I cleanse the wound, remove the thorn and go on. The infection heals, the skin grows over and all is well. Do you follow?'

'Yes,' the boy answered.

Atman nodded and smiled. 'Simon, you have such a thorn embedded in you. Not in your flesh, but in your mind. Your memory. And there it lingers – unremoved, uncleansed, unhealed. Secret still. Tell me about your thorn.'

The boy was silent.

'Perhaps I ask too much. Perhaps I ask too soon. Tell me first of Aquila and its flight to the sun.'

'It flew too close.'

'And . . . ?'

'Its eyes were burnt out.'

'And . . . ?'

'It fell to the earth. To be renewed again.'

'Good. Now, tell me of your poison thorn, if you are to truly see.'

The boy turned away.

'Last night, on the summit, you made a claim on yourself. I know it. It is the way of the bird. Would you deny that claim so soon?'

Simon lifted his head, squarely facing the man. 'No, I wouldn't.'

'Then I am listening.'

'But I've never told before. Not anyone. Ever.'

'Which is all the more reason to tell me.'

The boy sighed and looked away, then back, just as squarely. 'I was little. Only five. It was dark and I was playing in the street. I was alone. Other boys came out of the darkness. They were bigger than me. Much bigger. Strange boys I didn't know. And because I was so small, and by myself, they picked on me. Teased me and chased me. To beat me up. So I ran. I zigzagged down streets where I'd never been before. Into alleys. Into the dark. To hide . . .'

'They followed you?'

'I think they did. I don't really know. I think I heard, but I didn't look. And when I did – just once, when I turned – I fell.'

'And?'

'That was when I lost my eye. There were bushes. Dead branches on bushes, all white and hard, bony, and one of them . . . one of them went in. Stuck in my eye and broke off. I pulled it straight out, but I couldn't see. Couldn't see anything. There was blood. Awful black blood. Thick.

Everywhere. All over me. And dark. Everywhere was dark. It was terrible. Terrible . . . All because I was gutless. A coward. See?'

'I do,' Atman answered. 'So will you, now.'

Only then did Simon smile. 'Thank you,' he whispered. 'I know that I will. Thank you.'

'Now hold me, once, before leaving,' Atman asked. 'And do not fear. The way that I am taking is not dark. I move into the light. A universe of light. Should you need me, you will find me. In your heart – even as Altair is at the heart of Aquila – I will be there. There you will see me. Through the eyes of the heart.'

When he was silent the boy knelt and held him and after, without a word, he left him to be.

24 October

My dear Shane, well, the rains have certainly set in. As long as we don't get bogged, and I know that I have some dry clothes to put on at the end of the day, I can enjoy the change from the heat. The camels seem happy with the rain as well. We're taking them back to the mine for McTaggart, at Atman's request. I'm making the most of the ride. The others prefer to walk. Greg is at the front, leading the way, while Simon is trailing behind. Each one of us seems to be in a world of our own.

Atman insisted on staying where he was. I was uncomfortable about leaving him there, but I felt I had no right to dictate to a man who is facing the last hours of his life. I think he will die very soon. How can you argue with a dying man's wish?

We managed to make it out of the crater just in time. Apparently the rain that falls in the surrounding hills is funnelled down through that one passage Atman called the Needle's Eye. When we came through, the water was already over our ankles and flowing fast. The high water mark on the wall was three metres!

I have been sitting here, rocking gently on the camel, with its slow comfortable gait, and thinking. Thinking about my grandmother and about the Wazo – and about myself.

Do you know of any culture, at any time on earth, which didn't have its own stories? My grandmother and I have grown up in different cultures and so we've acquired different stories – her culture's stories are mainly myths. She speaks of Brahma, Siva, and Vishnu representing the notions of creation, disintegration and preservation, respectively. Facts of life that are eternal. Vishnu has a consort, Lakshmi. She represents wealth, which I understand to be the abundance and experience that comes hand-in-hand with life.

My stories are called 'science'. After what I've been through, I can't say if they're any more truthful than myth. Science is also forever changing and developing its stories. I'm not sure whether it was the myth or the science that caused me to come and search for the Wazo. They both inspire us to act, and both are ways of explaining our lives. But it seems to me, only myth offers the dream of what could be.

As a child I remember my grandmother telling me that we are never alone. That sounded silly to me then. How many millions of Garudas would there have to be to spy on every one of us? Now I realise the truth of the statement. We all have to learn from our experiences. We all have to question ourselves because we all make mistakes. We are all discovering our own track through life. And I'm coming to realise that finding the truth behind a 'fact' is OK, but not as rewarding as finding the truth within ourselves.

So, I also need to speak truthfully to you about the Wazo. If what I experienced last night was a dream and I write the article that I had planned about the myth of the Wazo, with photographs of the sites where it was supposed to have been encountered, I won't have proved anything; certainly not its existence, nor that it exists solely in people's imaginations. In spite of what I write, the myth of the bird will continue, and the exposure might even encourage more people to believe.

But if I wasn't dreaming when I saw it, and the bird is a new species, significantly larger than any other living today, then I have two possible responses. I could say nothing in an attempt to keep it hidden and allow the future of the species to take its natural course, to thrive or perish.

On the other hand, I could write an article detailing what I saw, with photographs – very blurred under those conditions, if they come out at all! Breaking the story of a new species of raptor would be great for the magazine. Great for you and for me, but what would happen then? Would conservationists and ornithologists have the political power to protect the bird's habitat and ensure its survival? That would involve people conducting studies and developing conservation and breeding programmes, like they have with the Californian condor. But scientists would certainly not be the only ones interested. I'm told that each time there's a reported sighting of a Tasmanian Tiger, hundreds of people gather, some to look, but some with rifles ready! And there are those who would want to make money out of it. A bird with such romance as the Wazo could make someone a great deal. I'm sure some egocentric collector would be willing to pay a high price on the black market to keep one as a prized possession.

Before I decide how to present this story, what point of view to take, I need to be clear what I'm wanting to achieve. I know the world is constantly changing and plenty of species have become extinct without human help. I can't, and I don't want to, stop all the changes that are happening on this planet. But what strikes me as crucial is that we humans don't exist in isolation. I'm realising more and more that we live in an ecosystem that is complex and diverse and all its components play a part in some way. The more species that die off, the weaker our system becomes.

Shane, I know that in my little life I need people with a wide range of skills and values so that I too can live and produce – I need you and your staff, the many thousands of people who make my food and equipment, and I need people like Simon, Greg and Atman.
I couldn't survive without them.

So, right at this moment, I'm not sure what's the best thing to do to allow the Wazo, whether it's a myth or a scientific fact, its freedom.

Whatever I decide, I'm not going to rush into it, and what's more, you'll be the first to know. That's the best I can offer, right now.

To come back to a more personal topic, Greg asked me where I was planning to live after I've finished up at Esperance. He said that if I hadn't already committed myself elsewhere, he'd like me to come and stay with him at Deep River. I suppose it's obvious from what I've been telling you that things between us have settled down. I feel more comfortable with him, though I've no delusions that we've resolved all our problems. I told him that I'd like to visit him at the sanctuary very much; that I'm willing to give things another go and see what happens from there. As things stand today, I like the thought of spending more time with him – and Simon too, for that matter.

Anyway, I'll be seeing you soon, so we can have a proper talk then!

All my love.

P.S. I've got a suspicion that a different type of adventure could be waiting for me . . .

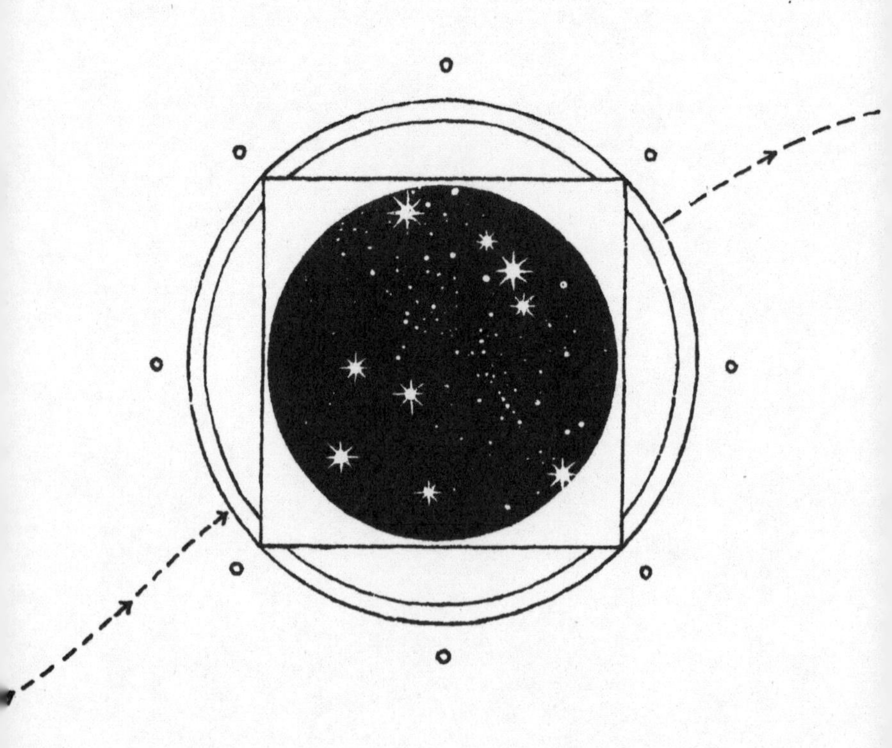

THE DRIVE BACK to Esperance was strangely quiet, the three being too preoccupied with their own thoughts, their own plans and resolutions, to speak. When at last they reached Mala's cottage it was as if they were different people from those who had left, hardly a fortnight before.

For Mala there was plenty to do – to such an extent that her priorities were divided: whether to develop the films that she had taken on the trip or to check on what had become of the ground parrot fledglings in her absence. In either case, she seemed eager to have her own space again, to be alone and *doing*, rather than sitting, talking or organising the other two, or having them 'under foot'. Not that she needed to worry about that.

Greg was eager to get away. 'There's the sanctuary,' he said, only half-apologetically. 'I have to get back. You know that' And while Mala had come to appreciate his company, she did not attempt to argue. It would be good for both of them to go their separate ways, for a while at least, although both understood – or intuited – that 'a while' might be little more than weeks. If that.

Simon had his own agenda too, although he kept it to himself, as always.

They arrived at the cottage late one afternoon and used what little daylight was left to unpack the car. Mala found some pasta in her pantry and, after eating, each disappeared to bed as if by magic.

The next morning was a different matter. When Mala came out onto her verandah, there was Simon, coffee in hand, to all appearances waiting for her.

'Hey,' she said, shoving her hair behind her ears in an attempt to look respectable.

'Hey, yourself,' he answered. 'Did you sleep OK?'

There was something about his unfeigned brightness, the sheer pleasure in his smile, that she could hardly believe. For nearly four days he had sat, quietly brooding, and now this.

'Yes, I did, thanks,' she said. 'And you?'

'Like a baby.'

She had to laugh. Nobody looked less like a baby than he did. Once she had seen him as a boy, but now – as if scales had suddenly fallen from her eyes – she saw a man.

A young man, but a man all the same, and a happy one. And a good-looking one at that.

'So,' she said, 'feeling pretty fine, are we?'

'Yep,' he nodded, taking a sip of his coffee. 'That's why I was wondering, before Greg gets up, if we could take a bit of a walk on the beach, just the two of us. Up towards Mississippi Point. For old times' sake.'

She felt a lump rise in her throat when he said that. Not just because it did seem so long since they had been there together, but because he should actually ask. 'Why?' she said. 'Is something wrong?'

He put his cup down on the verandah rail and turned to her, all smiles. 'No, the opposite, I'd say. So, do you want to?'

How could she refuse him?

They walked in silence to the water's edge and then turned east, into the sun, the brisk morning waves breaking around their ankles.

'Mala,' he began, 'I just wanted to thank you. You know, for letting me come with you. For putting up with me. I guess I don't really know what else to say, even though I've been thinking about it for days, if you know what I mean . . .' and he trailed off, looking out to sea to hide his embarrassment.

Mala struggled to collect her thoughts. Saying goodbye to Greg was one thing – they went back a long way – but to Simon . . . 'You've got nothing to thank me for,' she finally managed. 'If anyone behaved like a jerk, it was me. I'd say that I threw as many tantrums as you. And I'm, well, a bit older than you, and should have known better. So, if we're into apologies, I'd like you to accept mine, too.'

'Sure,' he muttered. 'But I was your guest and I should have behaved.'

When he said this she stopped and put her hand on his shoulder, turning him towards her. 'Simon,' she said, 'this is silly. We both had a lot to learn. We both still have a lot to learn. That's what it means to be a human being. Well, one who's truly *alive*, it seems to me. Truly *growing*. And we've both done a lot of that. At least, that's the way I see it.'

'I know,' he agreed. 'But you, I thought that you were always terrific. Right from the beginning. The first time we walked along here, and you showed me the parrot fledglings. Jeez, they were minute compared to the . . .' but he stopped himself from finishing, from mentioning the bird. He knew too well that this was a private experience, one that he had no desire to share, nor would he expect her to. What they had seen, they had seen. That was that. So he changed the subject. 'I've got something for you,' he said, and he reached deep into the pocket of his jeans. 'I never gave a girl – a woman – a present before. Or a gift, as Atman would call it. You won't laugh, will you?'

She was too stunned to do anything; all the more so when he took her hand and pressed into it a deep blue stone, rough and round, like a pebble.

'It's an uncut sapphire,' he explained. 'Old McTaggart gave it to me when you were hobbling the camels. I hope you like it. I thought maybe, if you and Greg ever, you know, got hitched, you might . . .' But before he could finish she had pushed him into the surf, where he rolled, laughing and splashing, until she was drenched herself.

By midday, when the farewells were over, Greg and Simon left to head back to Deep River. At least that was the man's intention, but he had calculated without the plans of his companion. Little was said until the outlying buildings of Esperance came in sight, then Simon turned from the window and cleared his throat, leaving no doubt that he had something to say, and was waiting for an invitation.

'I'm listening,' Greg encouraged him. 'And have been for the last few days.'

Simon laughed. 'Well, that's too bad,' he said, 'because I haven't had anything worthwhile to say until now.'

'Then fire away. Tell Uncle Greg what's on your mind.'

'It's not so much that I've got something to tell you. But there's some questions.'

The man took his eyes from the road, genuinely surprised. 'Something to ask me? Since when did you take my advice?'

The boy shook his head. 'No, it's not advice that I want either. It's information. And a request. OK?'

'I'll do my best.'

'First, there's something I don't really understand. Something I need to know. Since the beginning, way back at the sanctuary, when you showed me those photos on your office wall and talked about finding the bird, well, that's all you wanted to do. You said you had wanted to for years and years, but then, that last night with Atman, when you could have, you wouldn't come. I don't get that. I just need to know.'

The man was silent then, thinking, until finally he said, 'Will you answer a question for me first?'

'I'll try.'

'Then tell me, would you have had to see it, the bird, before you believed it existed?'

Now the boy was silenced. He turned away, back towards his window. 'Before I saw it, yes. But now, knowing myself better, like I do, I guess not. No.'

'And why's that?'

'Because . . . because the bird is . . .'

'Yes, the bird is, I'll give you that. But what is it, exactly?'

The boy sighed, wrestling with himself, deep inside. 'Because the bird is . . . different things to different people. Like a symbol . . .'

'Go on. A symbol of what?'

'Of life . . . that's what it is. A symbol of promise. Life's promise.'

'And?'

'The gifts that life holds. If we look out for them. If we search for them. Inside ourselves. Until we find them.'

'Do you think we'll find them all? These gifts?'

'Maybe not. But it's the trying that matters. The searching.'

The man nodded slowly. As he did, the boy saw in him – caught in him, momentarily – the face of Atman, and his *knowing*.

'Now,' Greg said, 'you might answer your own question. Why didn't I need to see that bird? Why did I stay behind?'

'Because you already knew. Because to see, with your eyes, what you already knew, wasn't important. So you stayed with Atman because you knew that he was dying, and, right then, that's what really mattered. That has to be the reason.'

'It was, although I don't always practise what I believe, which is part of being human, as you'll find out. Anyway, there you go. You answered that one yourself. But there was something else? A request, you said?'

Now they were passing through Esperance itself, and Simon didn't hesitate. 'Greg,' he said, 'I want you to drop me off here, in Esperance. At the museum. Will you do that?'

Greg shrugged. 'Sure, no sweat. How long do you need?'

Simon shook his head. 'No, I don't mean to wait for me. I mean to leave me there. All right?'

'No, that's not all right. I made a deal with Graham and Burwood that I'd get you back safely. And that's what I'm going to do.'

Simon turned to the window again, smiling a deep and secret smile. 'Well, then,' he said, 'would you rather that I shot through the first time you stop to get fuel? Because that's what I'm going to do. And then you'd really have egg on your face . . . *and* all over your report. What about that?'

'You wouldn't. Not now.'

'Greg,' he said, turning back, 'you just don't get it, do you? You take me back to those guys and I'll be no better off than I was before – no matter what you say in your stupid report. They'll say, "Hey, thanks, Greg. You did a really good job on a hard case. Now, how about you hand him back to us." And you know what will happen then? I'll get pissed off to some other scheme for losers. Some other Endeavour Programme or whatever else they call it – they're all the same.'

'They're not. And it won't be like that. Not after what I tell them.'

Simon sighed. 'They *are* all the same, and you know it. You're never *forgiven*. Nobody ever really believes that you can change. Tell me I'm wrong.'

Greg was silent. In all honesty he couldn't assure the boy of anything. Least of all the outcome of his report; not even the fact that it would be read.

'So,' Simon went on, sensing the glimmer of victory, 'I'm asking that you let me out here. Don't force me to run. Just let me go, and tell them that you did. And why.'

'Maybe that's what you should be telling me,' Greg remarked dryly. 'So that if I do, I get my reasons right.'

'Because I want a real chance to prove myself without shooting through like a coward. On the sly. Because of all the things I just told you. All the things that I've learnt from Mala, and you, and Atman, and everybody else who helped me to find out who I really am. Who I might be. Even Graham and Burwood gave me a backpack – and that was a gift, see? I just have to try, by myself. I know that I can make it. I just know it. That's what I found out, up there, with the bird. That I could. I will . . .' Here he stopped, afraid that he had said too much, and he turned to the window again, to hide the tears of frustration that were welling within him.

But Greg understood. 'At the museum?' he asked. 'Why there?'

Simon wiped his eyes with the back of his hand. 'I can't say, exactly. But Atman told me about this old woman called Dr Gwen. She was the one Mala interviewed there. She gave Mala the knife that was passed on to me. She was the one who slipped the feather into Mala's camera bag. Atman and her were pretty close. They both knew things about the bird. Even about me, somehow. Like they were expecting me. Waiting for me to turn up. Intuition, you could call it. I don't know. But I want to meet this Dr Gwen. Maybe even put in some time at the museum. Give them a hand there. Mala told me a fair bit about the place. It's like a time capsule. There's all this space junk from a satellite that crashed in the desert. I'd like to see that, to try and make some sense of it. Maybe do up a display. You know, like a view of the heavens . . .'

'What, like paint a backdrop?'

'Something like that.'

'Of a constellation, in the night sky?'

'Yeah. Like Aquila. You know. With this satellite, mounted, as if it was moving in front of it. Yeah. Something like that.'

'What about money? And accommodation? What about that?'

Simon pointed through the windscreen. 'I'd say there's your answer.'

Fifty metres ahead was the museum building and there on its front steps stood an old woman, her hand raised to protect her eyes from the afternoon glare, staring directly towards them. 'I reckon that's Dr Gwen. I'd say she's waiting for yours truly. What more do you want to know?'

'Nothing,' Greg laughed. 'Absolutely nothing.' And he pulled into the kerb.

If you would like to find out more about Hachette Children's Books, our authors, upcoming events and new releases you can visit our website, Facebook or follow us on Twitter:

hachettechildrens.com.au
twitter.com/HCBoz
facebook.com/hcboz

A chilling, intriguing story from one of Australia's most acclaimed authors.

On 4 June 1629, the Dutch vessel *Batavia* struck rocks off the West Australian coast. By the time help arrived, over 120 men, women and children had met their deaths – not in the sea, but murdered by fellow survivors.

Nearly 400 years after this atrocity, teenager Steven Messenger discovers gruesome relics from that wreck. Four months later he disappears without a trace. Where is Steven? Is his disappearance linked to the relics? Someone knows . . . somewhere . . .

Winner of the CBCA Book of the Year Award
Winner of the Victorian Premier's Literary Award
Winner of the NSW Premier's Literary Award
Shortlisted for the Edgar Allan Poe Mystery Fiction Award

'This stunningly original work defies easy categorization as it spins dual story lines into one spellbinding yarn . . . Crew tantalizes to the very end, leaving readers to speculate enthusiastically on the riddles he craftily leaves unsolved. His tale will electrify his audience.'

— *Publishers Weekly*

'*Strange Objects* will continue to tease and perplex readers of all ages long after it has been read.'

— *Australian Book Review*

'A supernatural mystery of a high order.'

— *Kirkus Reviews*